# INTOXICATING!

BY
KATHLEEN O'REILLY

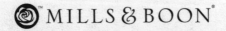

All the characters in this book have no existence outside the imagination of the author, and have no relation whatsoever to anyone bearing the same name or names. They are not even distantly inspired by any individual known or unknown to the author, and all the incidents are pure invention.

First published in Great Britain 2009
Harlequin Mills & Boon Limited,
Eton House, 18-24 Paradise Road, Richmond, Surrey TW9 1SR

© Kathleen Panov 2008
(Original title: *Sex, Straight Up*)

ISBN: 978 0 263 87492 1

14-0909

Harlequin Mills & Boon policy is to use papers that are natural, renewable and recyclable products and made from wood grown in sustainable forests. The logging and manufacturing processes conform to the legal environmental regulations of the country of origin.

Printed and bound in Spain
by Litografia Rosés S.A., Barcelona

**Kathleen O'Reilly** is an award-winning author of several romance novels who is pursuing her lifelong goal of sleeping late, creating a panty-hose-free work environment and entertaining readers all over the world. She lives in New York with her husband, two children and one rabbit. She loves to hear from her readers at either www.kathleenoreilly.com or by mail at PO Box 312, Nyack, NY 10960, USA.

# There was a Greek god sitting on her beach.

And as Catherine looked out the window of her house, in the tony Hamptons, the beach was everything ever painted by a master.

From her side angle, she could see him only in profile. A hard jaw that looked chiselled instead of real. He had forgone sunglasses, staring sightlessly into the churning grey waters of the Atlantic, with the sun burnishing him in gold highlights. His hair was short and dark, with a few pieces curling waywardly at the neck. Thick black lashes were clearly visible, even from a distance.

And that was only above the shoulders. His torso was like exquisite marble – powerful and broad, a sheltering bulkhead in any storm, its long axis divided by rippling abdominal muscles. A sprinkling of chest hair formed a narrow line down the sternum, leading to…to… Catherine smiled to herself.

There was art, and then there was *man art*.

Dear Reader,

This is a story that's been in my head for a long time. We were living in Texas on September 11, and I shared the same sad reactions as everyone else about the day, but the lives of those who died took on an equal and overwhelming significance, as we ended up moving to the suburbs outside New York City in December 2002.

Once my son started playing baseball, I attended many games at his school, and noticed a plaque. It's small, bronze and nailed up on the old wooden wall of the field house. It's in memory of a gentleman who was on the baseball board for the town and who died on September 11. It doesn't talk about the attacks, doesn't say how he died, but instead the words are about his life and his contributions to the league. In that moment, what had been such an infinite and nearly unimaginable tragedy became very, very real.

One life. One normal man coaching on this half-pint baseball field, who hadn't expected to die so soon, and the people he touched. Not an entire country, not an endless news clip circling many, but one family and one small community coping with the loss of a single person, amidst the tragedy of so many.

Respectfully,

*Kathleen*

## 1

—

SINCE THE SUMMER he turned eleven, Daniel O'Sullivan woke up every morning the same way. With an aching hard-on. After he was married, the first light of dawn became his favorite time. He'd roll over, impatient hands searching for his wife. After making love to her, he'd shower, shave, and together they'd take the subway to work. What more could any guy want?

But then one September morning seven years ago, bright sunlight mocking in the sky, that all exploded, along with two airliners, two buildings and two thousand, seven hundred and forty people—one of whom was his wife.

*Gone.*

For the next five years he rolled over to look for her, impatient hands searching blindly, and she wasn't there. And so the hard-on stayed.

The morning wake-up call evolved, the change coming so gradually that initially he didn't notice it. In those beginning moments of wakefulness, when his brain was more than half-unconscious, he stopped looking for his wife, impatient hands no longer reaching for someone who wasn't there.

*Gone.*

Daniel was starting to forget.

Now, if this was any of a thousand other people in the world, maybe that'd be okay. But Daniel wasn't wired that way. Love was forever. A promise was forever, and so two years ago he shifted the wedding picture to his nightstand as a reminder of exactly how much his wife meant to him.

It didn't help.

No matter what he did, no matter what he told himself, in those first seconds of the day his hands stayed stubbornly buried under his pillow. That betrayal to her memory shocked him as badly as her death.

And so the hard-on stayed.

Daniel didn't look at other women, he didn't flirt with other women and he sure as hell didn't sleep with other women. Maybe his sleep-bagged mind would betray her, but his body wouldn't.

His wifeless life settled into a dull pattern that he didn't dare disrupt. And it was for that reason that when summer rolled in to Manhattan, Daniel didn't leave like so many other New Yorkers.

July in Manhattan was hell. Hot, humid, and the dense air hung low on the rivers, casting the entire island in a muggy shade of yellow. The hell-like conditions were the number-one reason that most sane people left the city for the veritable paradise of the outlying beaches. The hell-like conditions were the number-one reason that Daniel O'Sullivan was determined to stay, no matter what his two brothers wanted.

"I'm not going," he told Sean and Gabe in his most serious, "don't hand me that crap" voice. And in case they didn't pick up on *that* completely unsubtle hint, Daniel turned back to the ghostly glow of the computer screen, ignoring them. They didn't usually gang up on him—actually, up until this point, it'd *never* happened before.

Stubbornly, Daniel scanned the bar's monthly spreadsheet, his eyes moving back and forth over the numbers with appreciation for such simplicity. Invoices and deposits showed a nice, tidy bottom line in the black. All in all, excellent news.

The bar currently known as Prime had sat on the corner of 47th and 10th for almost eighty years, and had been run by an

O'Sullivan equally as long. Gabe ran the place now, with Sean and Daniel as near-silent partners, except on Saturdays when the three O'Sullivans all worked there—Gabe and Sean to bartend, and Daniel to do the books.

After their uncle, the previous owner died, Gabe had paid up the back taxes on the place, against Daniel's advice. A bar in Manhattan was a shaky financial investment, but Gabe wasn't guided by business sense, but more by the desire to see the family legacy restored to its old grandeur. Against his own better judgment, Daniel had set up a desk and computer in the storeroom downstairs, so he could help with the accounting. The tiny storeroom was barely designed to accommodate one person. When you put three full-grown men in there—like now—the tiny quarters were stifling.

"It'd be good for you to get out of the city, meet some people," said Gabe, leaning back against a tall stack of cases of rum. Gabe, the youngest of the three, was a great bartender—a people person who never quite got the concept of being alone.

"And you could get laid," contributed Sean, in his own special way. Every man had one gear—sex—but wise men learned at an early age that you had to keep that fact hidden if you wanted to avoid complications in life and love.

Sean had the exact opposite approach to Daniel. With women, he was honest and up front about his sexual needs, and didn't try to apologize for it. Illogically, women never seemed to mind, which Daniel had never understood. Maybe it was Sean's law school diploma, maybe the planets had been aligned at his brother's birth. Daniel didn't know, didn't lose sleep over it, but there were times—like now—when Sean's "I know everything" attitude could be a complete pain in the ass.

"You haven't had sex since Michelle died, have you?" asked Sean, highlighting the mix of his lawyerlike interrogation skills and his general knack for the truth, tact be damned.

Gabe glared at him, so Daniel didn't have to. "You said you'd handle this with sensitivity."

"That was sensitivity," defended Sean. "I could have gotten a lot more graphic and reminded him about what he's been missing out on, but I took pity."

"Get the hell out of here," ordered Daniel, but neither of his younger brothers moved. At one time, they'd listened to him, obeyed him and respected him. One more thing that changed after 9/11.

How soon they all forgot. When Gabe joined Little League, it was Daniel who taught him how to pitch a fastball. And when Sean went off to college, it was Daniel who had explained all the knobs and buttons on the stove and dishwasher, respectively, without once making fun. And this was the thanks he got for keeping a straight face the whole time?

Daniel turned back to the computer. At least *it* didn't nag him.

Sean reached around his brother and turned off the monitor. "I think you need to rethink this monk strategy, Daniel. It's not working. You're tense. You're somber. Think back to the old days when you were—"

"Tense and somber," Gabe pointed out.

"It's none of your business," snapped Daniel, not looking up from the blackened screen. Usually teasing didn't bother him, but whenever the calendar moved closer to September, something hot, humid and hell-like rose up inside Daniel.

"You can't spend your whole life locked away," said Gabe quietly. "Besides, it's only one weekend."

The "weekend," as Gabe so politely phrased it, was a summer share in the Hamptons that Sean had rented, along with ten other lawyer types with too much cash and too much free time on their hands. There would be tanned, curvy women spilling out of bikinis, and eye-crossing amounts of alcohol. It was a more adult, socially acceptable version of Spring Break.

Only in New York.

Daniel shook his head, powered back on the monitor and then went back to work. Freezing them out usually worked, and he assumed that was the end of it, until Daniel heard light footsteps on the stairs.

Then, Gabe's girlfriend, Tessa, appeared.

His brothers had brought out the big guns.

Daniel silently swore as Tessa squeezed in next to Gabe, blocking his last escape route.

"You have to go, Daniel. I need you to check out a place about a mile down the beach."

Tessa talked with a soothing voice, her eyes so innocent and guileless, compared to his two more Machiavellian brothers. "I think it'd be perfect for one of my clients, but to get a feel for the place, you really need to be there and see it during the day and night. It'd be a great favor if you could do this for me, Daniel. Please."

Tessa's business was real estate and she lived and breathed it like other people inhaled oxygen.

Ah, jeez. The walls were closing in, and Daniel rubbed a hand at the back of his neck, trying to act as if there weren't ten thousand needles sticking under his skin. It was one thing to turn down his brothers; it was another matter entirely to disappoint a woman. Out of the three O'Sullivans, Daniel was the polite one, the courteous one, the chivalrous one. Right now, he was the frustrated one.

"Getting your woman to fight your battles now, Gabe?"

Gabe pulled Tessa into the crook of his arm. "I'm not proud. It's one weekend, Daniel, not a lifestyle change."

"Why aren't you going, Sean?" asked Daniel suspiciously.

Sean still stuck by his story. "I decided it would be better if we shoved you out of the airplane, so to speak. A free-range opportunity to cut loose for a few days. You could use it, dude."

Daniel eyeballed his brother. If it'd been Gabe talking, he would have bought it, hook, line and sinker. But this was Sean. "What's the real reason?"

Sean slugged easily, knowing he was busted. "Ashley invited me to go to Miami. Meanwhile, the time-share group needs a guy to even things out. If not, I'll get blacklisted for skipping. There're statutes in place for summer shares and anyone who violates them gets kicked off the island. Since Gabe's off the market you're the only brother left."

Now *that* sounded like Sean. "I don't want to bail you out."

"I'm only thinking of you," his brother said, wide-eyed with innocence. A man who was exposed to perjury on a daily basis could end up with his moral compass adjusted.

Gabe coughed. "Don't lay it on too thick, Sean."

Sean's eyes narrowed. "You're going to sit back and let him rot down here? I don't know about you, but I want my brother back. Three years passed, and I kept my mouth shut. Five years passed, I kept my mouth shut. Now, seven years have passed, and I'm done keeping my mouth shut."

"And aren't we all grateful for that?" drawled Daniel, clearly surprised that Sean was getting this worked up.

Sean pointed a finger at him. "Shut up."

Even more surprised, Daniel did just that. He stared at his two squabbling brothers, rubbed his eyes and discovered a new and improved guilt—with extra ulcer-inducing power. He'd done this to his family. Three brothers. As such, they'd always stood together, supported each other, and yes, they fought, because they were normal, but not like this and not because of him. Daniel was the role model, the responsible one. Or he used to be. Like all the other changes in his life lately, that didn't sit well. He didn't want much. Mainly to be left alone, but he wasn't going to have his brothers fighting because of him, either.

"I'd be crap company," he said halfheartedly. Guilt did that to him. Made him weak.

Sean spread his hands wide, accidentally socking Gabe in the gut. "Nobody will notice. All of the guys are from the office. They don't know you. Frank is bringing in four babes from a publicity firm in Chelsea that he says are infinitely doable. They'll think you're all dark and brooding. It'll be great. One woman's crap is another woman's soul mate. Who am I to judge?"

*A soul mate?* Man, Sean must have been drinking instead of serving the alcohol lately. A man didn't meet soul mates twice in his lifetime. Some men weren't even lucky enough to have it happen once.

"I don't know," muttered Daniel, but dammit all, Gabe was looking all happy and pleased, and even Sean was starting to smile. Daniel realized how long it'd been since he'd made his brothers happy. It seemed like forever. Mostly, all he'd been doing was making trouble and sending them on late-night binge-busts to rescue him from anonymous bars around the city and beyond.

Gabe put up a warning finger. "There is one rule. You can't wear your ring, Daniel. Women who go after the rings…well, you're not going there."

"I'm not taking off my ring," protested Daniel, rubbing the heavy gold band like a talisman. It wasn't even old, or worn, the metal still brilliant and polished. Almost brand-new.

Tessa nodded. "Sean's right. You can't wear the ring. The women will think you're some sleazeball. It's three days, Daniel. What harm can three days be?"

Sean and Gabe, he could handle, but he'd never liked saying no to a woman. It didn't feel right. They were forcing him to say no to a woman. It was his Achilles' heel, his fatal flaw, and they knew it and were exploiting him mercilessly. It was there in Sean's smug, merciless smile, and Gabe's way-too-innocent puppy-dog look.

*Three days.* It was only three days at the beach.

Daniel stared at them—all that was left of his family, all banded together to put him through their own version of Hell in the Hamptons. And they thought they were doing him a favor?

Fine.

He'd go—with his ring well-buried in his duffel. If he went, it'd make Tessa happy, make Sean and Gabe happy, and then he could return to his well-ordered life, and they would all think things were getting better.

Not a problem.

THERE WAS A Greek god sitting on her beach. He'd been there for hours, nearly motionless in stark contrast to the MTV-worthy volleyball game being played out on the sand next door. In Catherine Montefiore's current dreary mood, maybe she was more open to twenty-first-century classical eye-candy, she couldn't be sure. But, as she sat there, glued to the window of her grandfather's beach house in the Hamptons, the visual was as arresting as anything ever painted by Hopper, Dali or Picasso.

From her angle, she could only see him in profile. A hard jaw that looked chiseled instead of real. He had forgone sunglasses, staring sightlessly into the churning gray waters of the Atlantic, with the sun burnishing him in gold highlights. His hair was short and dark, with a few pieces curling waywardly at the neck, daring any stylist to mar its perfection. Thick black lashes were clearly visible, even from the distance. Lean, angular cheekbones cast shadows on the hard lines below.

And that was only above the shoulders—and what shoulders they were. In Catherine's profession she saw nude men by the crateload, and she knew sculpted shoulders when she saw them. The hard plane of the trapezium sloped down to a marvelously projected deltoid. His forearms were balanced on his knees, showing off rounded biceps and triceps, not in the wimpy expressionistic manner, but crafted in the more vivid Hellenistic style. Stalwart, capable and brutally real.

With busy eyes, she studied all of him, tracing over the sinews and the tendons that visibly flared when he moved.

Her hands flexed, aching to study, and even more daring, to touch. Eventually, she was unable to resist any longer, and she pulled out her sketch pad and pencil, and her fingers flew, guided by equal parts artistic endeavor and lust.

As his shape began to reveal itself on the paper, she knew she was wrong. Gods were unmarred perfection. No flaws, no scars, all-powerful, all-seeing. This man wasn't a god, but a mortal, complete with the scars that sprang from humanity.

This man was Odysseus, searching for home so far across the sea. Feverishly she sketched in the face, drawing from perfect memory now. The forehead cast a shadow over the rest of his features, sadness inherent in his brow. She left the eyes for last because she couldn't imagine the loneliness that echoed there, desperate to see his family, the broad, capable arms so uselessly empty.

Her quick fingers sketched out his body, a warrior's body, but with him sitting in the deck chair, the anterior view of his chest—along with the complete view of his lower torso—was obstructed. Conventional wisdom said that she needed two yards between her and the subject. In this situation—solitary woman ogling strange man—two yards was too close, but she could do better than her current spot behind the windows. Quietly, she opened the French doors that led out to the wooden deck, careful so that he wouldn't hear and be disturbed.

The deck was small by Southampton standards. Four wooden Adirondack chairs, a green-and-white striped umbrella that shaded most of the area and a few plants scattered here and there. The plants had to be replaced on a regular basis because although there were many talents in the Montefiore family, a green thumb was not among them.

After settling herself under the umbrella and adjusting the chair to the locked and upright position, Catherine picked up her pad and pencil and stared out toward the western horizon. It was the innocent picture of a woman sketching the sun over the ocean—not a woman fantasizing about the man that was parked on her beach. Catherine tilted her head a mere twenty degrees westward, achieving the perfect view.

Her sigh was louder than she intended, but really, it couldn't be helped. His chest was powerful and broad, a sheltering bulkhead in any storm, delineated down the long axis by rippling abdominal muscles. His skin nearly bronze in the sun. Dark chest hair formed a narrow line down the sternum, leading to… Catherine smiled to herself. There was art, and then there was *man art*.

Guiltily, Catherine wiped away the drop of damning saliva that had dripped onto the sketch.

Catherine was nothing if not a product of her environment—her work environment, actually. Her grandfather was Charles Montefiore, owner of Montefiore Auction House, one of the nation's premier art and antiquities auction houses, thank you very much, and Catherine had worked her way up through the trenches. Starting as an assistant appraiser, then appraiser, and now she was an assistant to her grandfather on special projects, mainly high-profile auctions.

Not that she coasted on the family name, no way. Catherine had graduated with honors from Columbia with an undergrad and masters in art, yet in many ways she knew she was the disappointment in the family. She didn't have her mother's style, or her grandfather's showmanship. Catherine had attended Manhattan's most elite private school, summered in Europe, but a classical education didn't solve personality defects. Her mother called her an introvert; Catherine preferred the more elegant "reclusive artist," but technically both of them were right.

She studied the sketch in her hand with a critical eye. As an artist, it was the male form that captured her imagination. The power behind it, the strength of it, but unfortunately, most of the men she worked with were either gay or nearing retirement. Her exposure to rages of testosterone was limited to two-dimensional figures, flat and lifeless, and she liked the safety of the one-way relationship where she was in complete control. In the past eight years, she'd had two relationships in the accepted sense of the word. The one with Leon, which had sadly fizzled into abject nothingness because he was, well… blah, and the relationship with Antonio, which ended when he realized he was a woman trapped in a man's body.

After the Antonio fiasco, Catherine was faced with a choice. To be aggressive and search out single men in their natural habitat—bars—or resign herself to days spent appraising the male torso and nights spent dreaming about it. Catherine had wisely stuck with two-dimensional men on a sketch pad, or a canvas. It was easier on her ego.

While she was busy on her sketch, a bikinied blonde approached him. Catherine frowned because Odysseus should not be bothered by the obviously fake melons that were bobbing in front of his face. Thankfully, his expression didn't change when tempted by this modern-day Nausicaa, and the loneliness in his eyes stayed constant.

Classical baroque art would have been altered forever if some Hamptons Hussy had turned Odysseus into Mr. Happy-Go-Lucky Melon-Grabber.

No, Odysseus was worthy of so much more.

The blonde, not appreciating the rare masterpiece on the

sand, waved blithely and then flitted away. Eagerly, Catherine went back to her work, shading, erasing, sketching, correcting, until, at last, the piece was finished.

For a moment she was caught breathless by the image on the paper. It was good. Really good. A smile curved her lips because it wasn't something that she thought often. Even Grandpa would be proud of her for this one. Her sketches were a sideline brought on by too much exposure to great art, and too little talent to do anything serious with it. When you dealt with Van Gogh on a daily basis, Catherine's pictures of the male form resembled a kindergartener's. A talented kindergartener, but still—a kindergartner.

But not this sketch. This sketch was special. She had captured the solitariness of him, the weariness juxtaposed against the noble bearing. The more she looked at the man—the live man, not the two-dimensional likeness—the more she wondered about him. She'd never seen one human being stay so still for so long, a master of self-control. People in New York never looked lonely. It was, like, a cardinal rule of the city. How could you be alone with eight million other people? Yet Catherine knew it was possible. Maybe that was why the man intrigued her so. Maybe…

Unfortunately, if she kept this up, she was going to get caught, so she stashed her sketchbook away, pushed on her sunglasses and stretched her legs out in front of her. Finally, he moved, rising to his feet, and she drew in her breath. She was still smiling to herself when he turned around, and quickly her smile disappeared in case he mistook it for an invitation. Catherine wasn't built like the bikinied, sun-streaked blonde. She was a tall dishwater blond, fifteen pounds overweight on a good day, and she didn't even want to talk about the bad days. She only bought one-piece bathing suits that minimized her butt, which was where most of her weight settled when she overindulged in cupcakes—something she often did on her bad days.

He looked at her, his eyes skimming over her, not sexually, but automatically, taking in the details of his surroundings of which she was a part. She fought the urge to cover herself. Better to ignore him, as if he were a painting on the wall and nothing more. He paused, and she could sense the indecision, but then he walked forward—toward her.

As he moved closer, Catherine glanced down, making sure her sketchbook was lying innocently closed on the ground. Check. No reason to be nervous at all.

He approached her, bare feet sinking in the sand, and sadly she realized that even his feet were glorious. She'd never sketched a foot in detail before, but now she thought she might.

"I hope I'm not intruding," he said, and she shook her head as if he had hadn't intruded on her brain since she'd first caught sight of him.

"You're welcome to sit as long as you want."

When he was this close, she could see his eyes. A dark, rain-fogged gray. His gaze was detached, not in a cold way, but empty and lifeless like the people captured in paintings by Piero.

"I thought this place was empty, and next door's been a nuthouse," he told her, automatically endearing him to her because in her mind she *knew* next door was a nuthouse. Loud, laughing, filled with happy, beautiful people who splashed away in the pool. Yeah, right. When you worked in art, you learned that anything could be forged.

"Please, don't apologize." She spoke graciously, adapting the lady-of-the-manor poise of her mother. "It's not necessary. Stay."

Restlessly, he shifted on his feet, so staying didn't seem to be in the cards. She knew the stance. She'd done it often enough. The man was itching to leave her company, but he waited, as if he knew he was only three words shy of being polite. Again, all familiar territory for Catherine. "I'm Daniel," he said finally.

"Catherine." She lifted her hand to shade her eyes from the sun, which was totally a great idea because when she blocked out the glare, and the shadows fell across his face, he seemed more alive. And she could see the neat symmetry in his facial structure.

Oh, yeah, she was going to draw him. Capture the tiny dip in his chin, capture the stubble that dotted his jaw. Oh, yeah.

"Thank you, Catherine."

"My pleasure," she answered, because it was.

All polite obligations now out of the way, Daniel went back to his chair, and there he sat for several more hours until the sun set for the day.

Catherine stayed in the lounge, sipping on tea and pretending to doze, and not once did he go into the water.

# 2

THAT NEXT MORNING, after a mere three hours' sleep, Daniel rose, rubbing tired eyes. He'd forgotten the infinite joys of a summer share. The long hours of drinking, the bed-hopping, the endless unfunny jokes. In search of peace and quiet, he'd first tried sleeping on the lounge outside, but when Chelsea and Bill went skinny-dipping in the wee hours of the night, Daniel gave up, creeping over to Catherine's deck before finally settling into a deep sleep in one of the chairs.

Sean was going to owe him for this, and Daniel occupied those first waking thoughts creating endless painful punishments for his brother, almost all involving testicles being squeezed into a vise. Only two more days, he reminded himself, rubbing at the empty spot on his ring finger. Still that didn't stop the nightmares about losing it. With an empty ring finger, the hole inside him seemed impossibly bigger. Some things just weren't meant to be left behind.

After a long stretch, he walked back to the nuthouse and was safely on one of the summer share's loungers when Catherine emerged on her deck. She waved, he waved, and they ignored each other for most of the morning until some dipwad got the bright idea of tapping a keg on the sand, which he couldn't even do right. Daniel chose not to educate him on the finer talents of keg-tapping. That was long ago and far away. Instead he fled back to Catherine's beach, praying she wouldn't mind.

It took her an hour to approach. "You're having problems next door, aren't you?" she asked, collapsing down into the sand next to him.

Daniel laughed with little humor. "Yeah. I'd love to go home if I could, but the lawyers would report back to my brothers and I'd just have to do it again another weekend."

"The lawyers?" she asked, taking off her sunglasses.

"My brother's firm. Long story. You don't want to hear it."

She looked at him, looked out at the water, then looked next door. Eventually, she stared at him again, frowning. "Why *are* you here?"

"Not by choice."

"I can see that," she said, so quietly he almost didn't hear.

That was what he liked about her. Her quiet. Everything about her was designed to escape notice. Her swimsuit was nearly identical to the sensible one-piece she wore yesterday. Built for swimming, not for looks. Her blond hair was long and unstyled, falling past her shoulders. He didn't think she was wearing makeup, but Daniel was no expert.

Although he really liked her eyes. Without her sunglasses he could see that she had nice eyes. Big, brown eyes that watched him steadily…until he met her eyes, and then she blinked, looking away, a pale flush rising up her cheeks. Next door, one of the lawyers—Samuel?—chased a woman down the beach, until she turned and let him catch her.

Why did everyone have to be so damned loud? Daniel shook his head. He noticed Catherine watching the people next door. "You want to go over there?"

Quickly, she shook her head. "Oh, no. I'm comfortable here. What about you?"

"I'm happier from a distance. This way I get to study people."

"Ah, a zoologist," she said, her lips curving up for a moment.

"People are fairly easy to peg."

"Really?" she asked skeptically, pulling her legs up underneath her and digging her toes into the sand.

"Oh, yeah," he answered, as if he were the world's foremost expert at psychology. Gabe would have laughed his ass off, but okay, Gabe wasn't here.

"So tell me about the man in the blue swim trunks."

Daniel thought for a second. He didn't know these people well, but he knew the types by heart. "Anthony. He's a clown, goof-off, doesn't take anything seriously."

"What about the pale guy, the one who's going to be hurting from the sunburn tomorrow?"

"Bill. I think. William. Bill. Billy. Something. He's a little weird. Drinks too much. Works too hard."

"What about the girl with the dark hair under his arm?"

"Her name's Chelsea, ambitious, but does things with no half measures."

"So why is Chelsea, who does things with no half measures, wasting time with weird Bill, when she really wants Anthony?"

"No way," he said, but then he glanced over at Chelsea and realized that Catherine was right. Chelsea might be spending her nights skinny-dipping with Bill, but when Bill wasn't looking, her eyes were glued to Anthony. That didn't even make sense. "Okay, assuming that you're right—possibly. Then why's she wasting her time with Bill?"

Catherine moved her head, and her hair fell across her shoulder, following the blue fabric of her bathing suit, stroking along the curve of her breast. Daniel immediately looked back at Chelsea and Bill.

"She doesn't want to be alone, and she doesn't think Anthony will like her enough. Most people will latch onto anything rather than learn how to be by themselves."

"I didn't think that could be taught." He'd spent the last seven years alone and didn't have too many problems with it.

"I think so. It's a good thing to be comfortable with yourself, knowing what you're capable of, and what you're not. You don't have to waste so much time faking your way through life. Sometimes faking is worth the effort, but most of the time it's not."

The quiet voice of reason. Daniel liked her even more. "You do this for a living?"

"No, not even close," she said, laughing.

"So how come you know so much?" he asked, because she had noticed details he missed. Coming from an accountant, that was just sad.

"Like you said, people are easy to peg."

He looked at her again, checking for the details he might have missed. She surprised him, but in a good way. It wasn't that he was antisocial, it was mostly that everyone he met was chock-full of filler conversations that contributed absolutely nothing to anything—or so he thought. Yet here he was, having a filler conversation that contributed absolutely nothing to anything…or did it?

Catherine's theory explained a lot. Why Warren in the office took off every Thursday for drinks after work with Thom, when he couldn't stand the guy. Why Kim went to lunch with Madeline on Fridays, which was about the stupidest thing ever, since Madeline had taken Kim's job as operations manager. How hard was it to eat alone?

"You have needy friends like that, too?" he asked curiously.

"One friend who keeps seeing her ex, who makes her miserable." She leaned forward, her hair brushing over her shoulder again, down her breast. This time Daniel looked for a long minute before glancing away.

"Maybe she loves him," he said, his voice rough. The heat was getting to him, making him light-headed, his skin hot.

She slipped up her sunglasses, her feet digging under the sand until they were completely covered. "She doesn't love him. She doesn't even like him."

"People are strange," he said, looking away from her, focusing on the waves until his brain righted itself.

"Got that right," she agreed.

Their conversation drifted on from there, moving from one nothing topic to another, but he definitely liked this. As they talked, the sun shifted in the sky. Daniel leaned back in the chair, relishing the warmth of the rays that reflected off the water. All in all, it was definitely good. Definitely.

Eventually the conversation dwindled, and the silence fell, perfectly balanced to the soothing ebb and flow of the white-capped sea.

Catherine watched the waves lap up onto the beach, and then cleared her throat. "You're welcome to sleep here if you'd like."

It took a moment for the words to sink in and Daniel's brows shot up at the invitation, in shock, and more than a little fear. She couldn't have noticed. When it came to hiding things, Daniel was an expert.

Then Catherine glanced in his direction, caught his deer-in-the-headlights look and laughed, a gurgling hiccup of noise.

"Not that way," she told him. "We have a bunch of rooms, and I don't play volleyball, or much else. Your brothers would never have to know."

He sighed, a great explosion of breath. One bullet dodged.

"Nothing to be afraid of. I promise," she said, and he believed her. The offer was beyond tempting. Her beach house was a shining beacon of serenity compared to the reality show next door. As if God knew and was laughing, one of the lawyers pulled out a karaoke machine and cranked up the volume, singing bad Bob Dylan at the top of his lungs.

"I don't know. That'd be a big imposition on a stranger," he said, but he heard the longing in his own voice.

*Pleeb.*

"I'm actually not that strange," she answered seriously, which cemented his decision. Anything was better than ten thousand drunken choruses of "Just Like a Woman."

"You sure you don't mind?" he asked, not that he was going to let her back out now. She was promising him an escape from more late-night skinny-dipping and the now-permanent ridge in his back where the deck chair slats had eaten into it.

She shook her head, her hair falling again, and this time he didn't look at all. "I'm sure. I draw a lot out here, so if all you want to do is sit by the beach and stare into the sun, it's not going to bother me at all."

"You draw?" he asked curiously.

"Not well," she answered, pulling her sunglasses back over her eyes, but not before he saw the uncertainty flicker in them.

"Still, it's something," he said, trying to reassure her. She looked as if she needed reassurance.

"What do you do?"

"I'm an accountant."

"Exciting," she murmured.

Daniel managed a half smile. "Don't lie."

She looked at him, black lenses hiding her eyes. "Actually, it suits you."

"Most people say that as an insult."

"No, you're very quiet and thorough and intense. I think those would be good qualities for an accountant to have."

She sounded completely serious. "Still, boring is boring."

"Ha. Not likely," she said so skeptically that he had to look at her twice.

"What do you do?" he asked, thinking that if she thought accounting was exciting, her job must be a complete snoozer.

"Art appraisal."

Not a snoozer, not even close. "Now see, that's exciting."

"Yeah," she agreed happily. "It usually is. We discovered a lost Picasso last year."

"Now that's much better than accounting."

"But you love it, don't you?"

Daniel didn't try to lie. Truthfully, he did love his job. The world needed accountants, like they needed scientists and garbage collectors. "I'm not designed to do anything else. There's a balance to accounting. Very exacting, very precise. No room for error. At the end of the day, you know exactly where you stand."

She smiled then, and he noticed that she had a nice smile. A full lower lip, and even white teeth that hinted at years in braces.

"Why do your brothers want you at the Hamptons?" she asked.

"To have fun."

Catherine laughed. She had a nice laugh, too. Almost hesitant until she got into it and then the sound made him smile and want to laugh along with her, but he didn't. "I shouldn't laugh," she said, putting a hand over her mouth.

"No, really, I think you should."

"So you're going to have a miserable time and prove them wrong, aren't you?"

"It hasn't been bad," he answered honestly. Since he'd met her, he had liked sitting with her, talking, under no obligation to be funny, or witty, or charming, or any of those other sterling character traits that Daniel had long forgotten.

"I won't say anything to your brothers," she whispered.

"Thank you."

"So, do you do anything besides accounting?"

Daniel hesitated, because he didn't tell many people about the bar. There were expectations of a bar owner, more of the fun-loving, pleasure-seeking crap, and Daniel usually kept his mouth shut. But Catherine would understand. He knew it. She was the type of person who invited confidences, the type of person who didn't demand or judge, and it had been so long since he'd had an ordinary conversation. He was surprised that he remembered how. "I'm part owner in a bar."

The sunglasses came off again, and he wished she would leave them off; her eyes were strangely compelling. So completely content. "I've never met a bar owner before. You don't seem the type."

This time Daniel did laugh. "It's my brother. He's the type."

"Ah. Your family must be close."

"Family distance is highly underrated."

She smiled at him. "Spoken by someone who is close to his family."

"When they're not playing therapist."

"Do you want lunch?" she asked, and Daniel checked his watch. He'd talked with her for nearly two hours, and never noticed.

"I shouldn't impose."

"Puh-lease. You're my houseguest now. What sort of hostess would I be if I didn't feed you?"

"You have something beyond snack foods and beer?"

She raised her brows. "That bad?"

"Hmm, it's not, but I'm thinking your food is probably better."

Daniel pulled on his T-shirt and followed her through the French doors to the interior of the house. Once inside, he heaved a blissful sigh. Now this was a beach house. There was no television, no stereo, only a couch overlooking the windows, two dainty sticks of wood, which Daniel termed "female chairs," a wall of rare books and what he guessed was really good art on the wall.

"This is a great place."

"It's my grandfather's. I freeload often."

"I bet he doesn't mind."

"Nah."

She opened the refrigerator and stared inside. "Eggs, salad, tuna and some berries."

"Very sensible."

"I have cupcakes and chips in the pantry."

"I won't judge. I swear."

"Thank you. Actually, I shouldn't have them," she said, skimming her hands down over her hips. It wasn't a seductive move, but a self-conscious one. Daniel's gaze automatically slipped lower, following her hands, and he felt something stir inside him.

A momentary flicker of heat.

Daniel looked away, and Catherine never noticed.

After lunch was over, Daniel grabbed a paperback thriller and sat out on the beach while Catherine sketched. He was curious to see her work, but she didn't invite him to, and so he left it alone. He waited until there was a break in the karaoke next door, the lawyers driving off for dinner, and Daniel took advantage, grabbing his duffel.

No one had even noticed he'd been gone. Excellent.

When he walked through her French doors, bag in hand, she looked up from the book she was reading on the couch, as if he had disturbed her. Daniel didn't usually second-guess himself; he didn't have to. But this time, he did. "Are you sure you don't mind?" he asked.

"Are you kidding? Don't worry."

After that, he stopped worrying and simply enjoyed himself. Dinner was great, and afterward when the shadows of evening had begun to fall, Catherine broke out a bottle of 1982 Rothschild, pouring two glasses. "Grandfather's got a truly excellent cellar," she told Daniel. She sat next to him on the couch, curling her legs underneath her.

The wine seemed like the perfect ending to what had been

the best day he'd had in some time. Seven years, in fact. Next
door might have been When Good Lawyers Go Bad, but here,
with the steady sound of the ocean, the quiet of the house, the
easiness of her company, Daniel felt peace.

"This has been nice," he told her. "I appreciate it."

"You don't expect much. I like that," she said, lifting her eyes
to his, and Daniel promptly forgot what he was going to say.
It'd been too long since he'd been in such a close setting. He
could feel the heat under his collar, the slow pound in his blood
and the push of his cock against what had been a loose pair of
shorts until he had found himself fascinated by a set of wistful
brown eyes.

*Snap out of it, O'Sullivan.*

Even before he could look away, Catherine did. Time for bed.
*Alone.*

He took a deep sip of wine and then placed it on the table,
getting to his feet. "I think I'll go to bed. Sleepy. Tired. Didn't
get much sleep last night." He was rambling, pathetically rambling, but he needed to run and fast. The poor kid was probably
completely unaware of the ideas that were suddenly flooding
his brain.

Catherine uncurled herself from the sofa, and he found
himself staring down the front of her bathing suit, which, up to
this point, had been sensible and concealing. But now it wasn't,
nope—when a man was staring straight down her front, he saw
flesh. Soft, pliable flesh. Soft, pliable bare flesh.

She lifted her gaze again, sending a shockwave through him
for absolutely no reason, because it wasn't as if she was going
triple-X on him. No, this was just her being her, and he was
suddenly in danger of busting a seam. For nothing. Just a set
of dark eyelashes. And the breasts. The soft, pliable…okay, it
was really time to leave. Past time to leave.

Daniel told himself to move, but it was too late. He'd found bottles of whiskey that were easier to escape than one single, soulful pair of shadowy brown eyes.

She rose from the couch.

His breathing stopped.

And then she kissed him.

# 3

DANIEL PULLED AWAY from her. "I should go," he said, completely and utterly embarrassing her.

Oh God. She had thought…well, who cares what she thought? She'd been so caught up in the rare moment of being in the close proximity of such a man-man and now she'd blown it. Why the heck did she think he'd want to kiss her?

Talk. Yes. Sex. *That's a big No.*

"I'm sorry. I shouldn't have done this. *Stupid, stupid, stupid.*" She was rambling. Whenever she got embarrassed, she developed a severe case of foot-in-mouth disease, which was a reason she always managed to avoid embarrassing situations.

"It wasn't that stupid," he answered, his eyes crinkling up nicely.

"I don't mean that it was stupid to kiss you, I mean, you're…" She waved a hand, searching for words, but found none, so opted for a silent adjective and stared a hole in the floor. He could figure that one out on his own. "I meant that I shouldn't have intruded into your space without an explicit invitation. It's rude."

"I didn't think it was rude," he answered evenly, making her like him even more. He was so polite, trying to make her feel better, and she did.

"Okay, maybe not rude, but wrong."

"It wasn't wrong, either."

"I shouldn't have done it. Let's leave it at that," she stated, trying to extricate herself from this with some pride intact.

"No, I think you should have done it."

At that point, as nice as his ego-bolstering was, she decided to bring him crashing back to reality. "Which is why I put the fear of God in you and you jumped?" she asked, as nicely as she could have when her words dripped with sarcasm.

He shook his head. "Not the fear of God. Something much more basic."

His voice changed at the end, turning rough and textured. In fact, she was so caught up in this newly discovered sexual-voice experience that she almost missed the words.

Almost. Her stomach pitched and then steadied, and she wondered if he knew what he'd just done. She didn't dare look up, but she sensed the change in the air. It wasn't the salt of the sea or the hint of black fruit in the bouquet of the wine. This was heady and strong, and sent bright bursts of fever rushing through her.

"So this is *okay?*" she asked, her breath thin and forced, coming from freshly squeezed lungs.

His hand curved around her waist, his fingers stroking softly, straying into the no-man's-land between her bare back and the elastic of her swimsuit. Her body shivered, nerve endings descending into pleasured chaos.

There was something so private, so personal about a man's and woman's gazes meeting, and Catherine didn't do it often. People thought she was shy, but cowardly was the better description. In her chest, her heart thudded painfully, and slowly, questioningly, her eyes raised to his, her Odysseus. Desire darkened the gray to black smoke, and he didn't look lonely. Not anymore. Catherine couldn't look away. Not now. Probably not ever.

Her hand reached out, touching the cotton shirt that covered his chest. One touch, to feel him. To touch him at last.

Her palm rested flat on him, over his heart, and she could feel the heated blood pounding there.

Warm flesh was so much better than art. The hard contours of his body weren't cold granite, or marble, but overflowed with muscle, bone and blood that called to her. She considered herself an expert on the male body in theory, but she wasn't even close when it came to the real thing. Right now, she was shaking like a kid. Gently, he inched her toward him, until her whole body was aligned with his, sternum to sternum, pelvis to pelvis, woman to man.

Bliss.

Then he lowered his head, covering her lips with his own.

Oh.

*Oh.*

She felt his mouth tremble, or was that hers? Catherine wasn't a virgin; she'd been kissed before, but not like this. Hesitation and reverence melted together under the heat in the air. Automatically she moved into him, his arms closing around her, wrapping her in twin bands of strength and steel.

Catherine sighed with relief, and when her mouth opened, his tongue eased inside, all hesitation gone. He stroked the inside of her lip, slipping back and forth until the drugging rhythm was ebbing through her blood, igniting her skin, pulsing between her thighs.

Her hands explored and she couldn't believe that this man, this masterful creation, was alive. A momentary doubt stole into her brain, but some things didn't lie, and the thick erection burning her thigh was proof enough. She wanted that proof inside her.

He broke the kiss, lifting his head, his breathing as ragged as hers, and she thought he was going to leave her.

"You'll stay with me?" she asked, needy, the doubts stealing back.

His face was tight with tension, his fingers biting into the curve of her hip, but she didn't care. She wanted his touch, and now the need overcame fear, overcame pride, overcame dignity. Her body needed this.

"Bed."

Catherine nodded because intelligent speech was impossible. She led him to her room, her nerves simmering, threatening to boil.

He was going to love her, touch her, kiss her, caress her, and she was dizzy with the thought of it. That amazing body that was currently hidden by his clothes was going to be hers. At least for one night.

"Can I undress you?" she asked, the words out before she could think, but how could she think? How could any sane woman think?

"That's what you want?" As if women didn't ask to undress him every day. *Heckuva job, Catherine.*

"I'm sorry. I shouldn't have said that." He was going to think she was obsessed. A nympho ready to pounce, and okay, she wanted him. Badly. But there were other forces at work inside her—namely the desperate desire to see him naked to know if her currently overworked imagination was right.

"Catherine, you don't have to apologize for everything."

"I'm— No, I'm not sorry. I wanted to see you because okay, this part *is* embarrassing, but not exactly for what you're thinking. You know that I draw, and, well—you have a perfect body for sketching." Her cheeks burned, and maybe now he thought she was weird, but weird was oodles better than sleazy.

"Really?" he said, as if he didn't think she was weird…or sleazy. In fact, he sounded…pleased.

"Absolutely. Certainly." And then, because he was watching

her so thoroughly, she drew his T-shirt over his head, struggling to be the artist she told him she was. "See this line here. It's the axis of your body, your dawn line, perfectly dividing the détente muscle, those are those…uh…little ripples." Her index finger traced the path, and she nearly sighed, but that would totally snooker the "dedicated artist" image that she was going for.

"I'll take your word for it."

"You should. I do this for a living."

"Really?" he asked, teasing her.

"Not this, but—" she drew a horizontal line across his shoulders, feeling the heavy muscles jump wherever she touched "—this."

Her palms felt the hard planes of his chest, absorbed the soft whirls of hair, the tight nipples, and she knew that she could never capture that vitality and strength on paper. Ever. Only in her hands.

She followed the trail of hair down, lower, and she knew the instant that he stopped breathing. Daringly, her fingers delved beneath his shorts, and then she stopped breathing, too.

But her curiosity wouldn't let her stop. Slowly, the soft boxers slid down hard thighs and then…

Then…

Oh, she wasn't going to look, but she had to look. She had to see, and heaven help her, she gasped.

Yes, like a total dilettante, she gasped.

For a second she could do nothing but gaze upon him with deep-seated lust, then her eyes studied his face.

He didn't look happy. He looked stressed.

"Can I see you?" he asked, and she nodded once before she realized that she needed to steer his expectations toward something resembling reality because she wasn't anywhere close to the perfection that he was.

"I'm not nearly as well-proportioned."

He drew down the straps of her bathing suit. "That's an entirely subjective statement. I think you're very well-proportioned."

"I weigh too much."

He slipped the suit off her hips and along her legs and looked at her for a long time, that comprehensive gaze making her nervous. He wasn't missing a thing. Not the half dozen cupcakes that resided happily on her butt, or her mushy thighs that didn't get nearly enough exercise or the pooch in her belly that four million sit-ups could easily cure.

"See?" she answered, completely sure he was going to tell her to put her bathing suit back on. In fact, she was so sure he was going to say that, that she reached down to pull it back over her mushy thighs, until he grabbed her hand in a death grip.

"Don't move," he ordered.

Catherine noticed the clenched jaw, the eyes that were mere slits of darkness, and began to relax. Eventually, his perfect chest heaved a sigh. "I'm better now," he said.

"You're nervous, too?" she asked curiously.

"Not at the moment. Tomorrow, yes. But right now, I'm good."

"I'm good, too," she answered.

His mouth took hers again, and he settled over her on the bed. There was another moment when his chest pressed into hers and he froze, and she swore that he was going to fly off her, but then he breathed again, and she sighed. It was very strange having a perfect man on top of her, his mouth kissing her, his hands touching her. But Catherine knew this wasn't a dream—the ache between her legs convinced her of that—and the way he touched her, almost desperately, convinced her of it, too.

She kissed him desperately, her curious fingers tracing the lines that she had drawn on paper, but the paper was cold compared to the warmth of his skin. No painter, no sculptor, no impressionistic master had ever captured that life, that heat.

She caressed the places that she had only imagined, and when she heard him groan, she smiled.

"I don't have a condom," he said, raising up on his arms. "I can't believe I forgot this."

*He was leaving her?* Hell, no. Instantly, pathetically, panic gave wings to her speech. "I'm on the pill. It regulates my periods. I have a heavy flow, my—"

Quickly, he shut her up with a kiss, and she really didn't blame him. Catherine curled her arms around his neck and breathed deeply. He smelled of sandalwood and wine, and she treasured that secret smell, locking the memory safely away. She would remember this. One stolen night that she would remember forever.

"You're sure?" he asked, and she could feel him, feel the hardness of him poised at her opening. More than anything she wanted to feel him there, inside her. She had to know how this would feel.

"Absolutely certain," she answered and the velvety hardness plunged between her legs. Once. Hard.

*Oh.*

Catherine froze.

"You're okay? I'm sorry. I'm rusty."

He sounded so apologetic, as if this was all his fault, and Catherine quickly moved to correct that heresy. "It's me. I wouldn't know if you're rusty or not."

He lifted up again, stared. "You haven't done this before?"

"Oh, yeah," she answered carelessly, like four times made her an expert, and Antonio hadn't been that good, but as her body adjusted, this felt…nice.

Daniel was large and bulky, and she loved how she didn't feel so tall when he was on top of her.

Again he began to move, with long, easy strokes, and she was fascinated with the idea of it, until it started to feel good—no, this was great.

Her hips followed his, melding together into this heady retreat and advance. Nervously, she met his eyes because he was so quiet. She found him watching her, those careful eyes looking at her face, her mouth, with a thorough intensity that almost frightened her, if it hadn't turned her on so much. All that—*for her.*

She felt his hungry gaze on her lips, wanted to feel his mouth, so she took a chance, kissing him, and…

It was exactly like before, his tongue teasing her mouth, seducing her lips, her skin, her entire being, until she couldn't think anymore, only feel. She grasped his broad back, the hard line of his buttocks, and felt him invading her, possessing her.

Oh oh oh…

Everything turned upside down inside her, and at the moment, Catherine realized why people loved sex.

This was heaven.

He thrust deeper inside her, plunging farther, moving faster, and her blood quickened. She could feel his muscles tightening, feel her own muscles clench and unclench instinctively, in a way that she had never known.

This was better than heaven. Oh, this was so much better than heaven.

Faster.

This was—

*Fasterfasterfasterfaster.*

Flying. She was flying now.

*Fasterfasterfasterfaster.*

*Ohhh….*

She couldn't speak, her brain liquid. Catherine's eyes popped open as the world began to collapse around her.

Then she felt his hand between her legs and the world didn't collapse, it exploded like a star, bursting into huge fiery pieces of color, and this from a woman who lived in a world of cream and beige and gray pencil slate.

Her thighs shook—in fact, her whole body shook.

No, he was shaking. Was he supposed to shake?

He cursed, but in a good way, she thought, as she felt him spill inside her. Warm, liquid, filling her.

Wow.

*Wowww....*

Then he collapsed on her, his back slick with sweat, his perfect chest expanding and contracting in great waves. "I'm sorry. That was too quick," he said, his face buried in her hair.

Quick? Quick? He thought that was quick? What happened when it wasn't quick? Good God, no wonder people got so heated up over this.

Her hand curved over his back, fascinated by the way the muscles bunched under her fingers. She loved this freedom to feel him, touch him, learn what the male body was truly like. In fact, she couldn't wait to draw him. Completely.

"I thought it was perfect," she said with a contented sigh.

He lifted his head, and when he looked at her, she saw something different in his eyes. The black had warmed to charcoal, his mouth curved up, smug with satisfaction. So often she'd seen that heady look staring back at her from a two-hundred-year-old canvas, or a black-and-white still photo, blind eyes that never saw her. But this man saw her.

"You haven't seen anything yet," he said, rolling off her to one side, and she missed that completeness, that weight pressing down on her.

"You're telling me this gets better?"

"Lots," he answered, stroking her hair. "It can be great, awesome, world-stirring."

"That's pretty impressive," answered Catherine, realizing that she wasn't a world-stirrer, and she wanted to be a world-stirrer. She loved this newfound lust for life rising up inside her. "Do you think we can make it to world-stirring?"

He smiled. "Yeah. I think we'll get there before the weekend is out."

And she snuggled into his chest, feeling the world transform from one-note sepia tones into full-blown impressionistic color, because before the weekend was out, they'd do this again, and Catherine's world was already starting to stir.

# 4

FOR MOST OF THE NIGHT, Daniel didn't close his eyes, but held Catherine tightly. It'd been so long since he held a woman in his arms. Forever. He didn't want to go to sleep because he was afraid he would wake up and be alone again. That this was all a dream.

He shouldn't have done this. He really, *really* shouldn't have done this, but there was something in her eyes that made "no" pretty well impossible.

And it was that knowledge that lessened the guilt. Yeah, he'd been a creep to take advantage of the situation, but there were words for guys who walked away when they were needed most. Daniel wasn't one of those guys.

From outside, the sounds of life began to stir. People would be waking soon, but everything here was so quiet, so peaceful. He didn't want to disturb it, he just wanted to live it.

In the city there was so much noise, and usually he liked the noise, since it drowned out the silence. But this quiet… For a second he listened.

The sounds of the ocean were so large against her quiet breathing, he felt her chest expand against his, the musky perfume of sex hanging in the air.

Man, what a marvelous smell. He hadn't known that he missed it until now. That smell, mixed with Catherine's smell—something soapy and flowery, but completely addictive.

Her bare thigh pulled up between his legs, brushing against

him, and he sprang to life, fully aroused and ready to go. She was sleeping so peacefully, and he didn't have the heart to wake her because that would be a selfish thing to do, completely taking advantage of the situation. But then she slid up his chest, her breasts pushing against him in a move that strippers would covet, and her eyes opened.

A lover's eyes, sly and sleepy.

Daniel knew that he couldn't live without seeing that look again.

He pushed inside her, saw her eyes go wide and felt a momentary pang of guilt, but then her lips curved, and her hair fell over his face, sliding across his cheek, and the guilt faded. The pleasure began.

THE SUN ROSE IN THE EAST, just as it always did. Daniel woke with an aching hard-on, just as he always did, but there was a woman next to him. A nude woman. A nude, sexually willing woman.

Daniel smiled and reached out a hand to touch her breast. She wasn't built like Michelle, who'd been short and slim, with what she termed "a lot of junk in her trunk," and Daniel could feel the differences.

Catherine was tall, with lush curves that filled his hands perfectly, hands that had never felt empty until now. In his opinion, she had the body of a goddess, earthy and rich, solely designed to give him pleasure. Her skin was the color of the morning sky at first blush, soft and warm.

His fingers caressed Catherine's nipple, feeling it react, and he wondered at that small miracle. A woman's body reacting. She sighed, her body arching into his hand as if it belonged there.

The sunlight cast a shadow on his empty ring finger, and he felt something stabbing at him, but he brushed it away. Not today. Today he was going to live. It was Sunday. His last day, and he wasn't going to miss this. When he left, he would bear the weight of the band again, but right now, he just wanted to live like a normal man.

Catherine woke as he imagined she did everything else. Slowly, methodically, with exquisite purpose. Her lashes moved, fluttered up, and then he found himself falling into her eyes once again. She was so soft, so uncomplicated, so irresistible.

He touched, circling her breast, feeling the constant beat of her heart. Her body tensed, still not comfortable with being nude, but he'd work on that.

*Whoa.*

Daniel frowned, and she touched his mouth. "Something wrong?"

He shook his head. "No."

*Today was it. Nothing more.*

"When do you have to leave?" she asked, reminding him exactly how much time he had left.

"I'll take the late train," he said, in absolutely no hurry to leave.

"Good," she answered, moving back the sheet. He had thought she was shy, but the odd thing about her? She seemed to love to watch his body, loved to touch his body, too, and jeez, what man in his right mind was going to object?

She traced a line down his chest, her eyes flaring dark. He loved to watch her, too, loved to watch her mouth grow slack with desire.

It had been so long.

His body jerked impatiently to life, and she smiled.

One day left.

Daniel didn't wait. He rolled over her, and drove inside, savoring that one second when everything within him converged to this single point, this single moment when his entire body came spluttering back to life, rough and cold and long unused—but not today.

The lashes fluttered closed, her mouth tense, and he watched her, watched the sun filter through the shutters, casting alternating lines of light and dark on her full breasts.

Daniel wanted to be in control of his emotions, wanted to be calm, easy. She needed that, but panic grabbed at him, sharp claws digging in deep.

*Just one day.*

One day before it all disappeared. Again.

So he thrust deeper inside her, her eyes focused on him, and he wanted to smile at her, wanted to act like everything was normal, but was it?

A rumbling sound came from low in his throat, a rough noise he'd never heard before. And he drilled inside her slick heat, until his mind was black, until his eyes were blind, because his body needed this.

It'd been so long.

His cock burned, the blood roaring through it like a fire feeding on air.

One day left. He moved faster, harder. Oh, he'd missed this. Harder, deeper, needing to touch her, needing to feel her, needing to… Breathe.

He needed to breathe.

He'd never used a woman like this before, not even Michelle. Daniel knew he shouldn't, but then Catherine's hands fastened on his shoulders, her teeth dug into her lower lip and her eyes flared with something dark and aware. It was the darkness in her that pushed him on. Raising himself up on his arms, he took. Oh, damn, he took. His head roared, louder and louder, until the pounding in his cock matched the pounding in his head.

Her head listed to one side, the tawny fall of her hair sweeping over the sun-gilded curve of her neck. Her body arched upward with each thrust, shuddering moans of pleasure escaping from her lips. Absorbing him, taking him…comforting him.

Daniel felt his body about to come, but he wasn't going to

do this alone. Not alone. He hated alone. He reached down and flicked against her. Found the place that she needed and watched her body buck.

He touched her, finding where they were joined, and his hand moved faster, and he kept thrusting inside her. She had to feel this. She had to feel the same hopeless need that he did.

Her teeth bit into her lip, and he noticed the blood.

"Come on, Catherine," he begged, because he needed her with him.

His hand moved, palm against her bone, and her eyes closed, her back lifted, and the moans grew loud and ragged. "A little more," he said, fighting back his release. She was close. He knew she was close.

She let out a cry, sounds stuttering, and her hips were sliding against him, against his cock, against his hand, until her body jerked once, her mouth opened and he couldn't resist.

He took her mouth, he took her body, and as the climax fell over them, Daniel surrendered to the darkness.

*One day left.*

CATHERINE LIFTED her head, stared and then fell back against the pillow. "I think the world was stirred."

"Thank God," he said, more of a prayer than a curse.

She reached out next to him and grabbed his hand, tracing over his palms, his fingers. He froze because it was wrong. He should be wearing his ring, but then Daniel forced himself to relax. To remember.

Gradually, the tension left and he closed his eyes.

"What do you want to do today?" she asked.

Right now, he would happily stay in bed all day, but that wasn't the politically correct thing to say, so he shrugged. "It's up to you."

"Could I draw you?"

"That's what you want?"

She nodded eagerly, and he knew he couldn't deny her even though the idea of being stuffed in some dainty French chair with his head twisted just an inch to the left would be hell.

"Okay," he answered, forced enthusiasm in his voice.

"Great." She rose from the bed. He watched as she covered her body in some shapeless bathrobe, and he felt a momentary sadness. For seven years, he had avoided thinking of female nudity, but now he was back into it in a big way.

Full, high breasts. Long, long legs that could wrap around him when he drove inside…

Daniel shook his head.

She flipped up the shutters on the windows, and the eastern light filtered in. "The morning light is the best," she told him.

Then she began to adjust him, staring with wide-eyed exuberance. His arm went this way, his head reversed, his fingers like this, and then she looked as if she would be adjusting him *there,* as well. He moved in and took control.

"What are you thinking about drawing?" he asked her carefully.

"Oh," she said, drawing the sheet back over him.

Instantly, Daniel sensed that he'd just missed something major. Some huge detail that he'd overlooked. When she looked at him again the exuberance was missing.

*Hell.*

"You want to draw me nude. Is that it?" he asked, because he'd never been exactly shy, but he wasn't Sean, either. Discretion. That's what he believed in.

Nudity was private, and sitting there bare-assed-naked while she sketched him…all while he wasn't supposed to be thinking about sex?

Hell.

"You don't have to. I don't want to make you uncomfortable. I'm around pictures of naked people a lot more than everybody else, and sometimes I forget," she muttered, her eyes resigned.

"All right," he said, throwing away every piece of dignity he'd ever had. The exuberance rushed back in her eyes.

The sheet went off, and she adjusted his thighs, his butt, his currently aching cock, and he gritted his teeth until she told him that he needed to relax his jaw.

*Easy for her to say.*

But eventually she quit touching him and went to work, sitting in a chair across from him, the sun at her back. Actually, it wasn't as bad he thought, because he got to watch her while she sketched him.

She was pretty. Really pretty, but it took someone with a careful eye to see it. The sun flashed gold in her hair, and when she got frustrated with herself, which seemed to be often, she would comb her fingers through the long strands.

At times, she looked, stared, watched him impassively, and he tried not to be affected. Unfortunately, when a woman watched his currently unclothed body with such single-minded focus, he couldn't help it. He hadn't had sex in a very long time and…well, there was a completely logical reason for a man to be aroused.

Heavily, painfully aroused.

Catherine didn't seem to notice, thank God. When she sketched, she got caught up in some other world that he wasn't a part of.

Her hand moved to the lower edge of the paper, and she leaned forward, the robe gaping an inch, almost enough…

If he moved his head only a fraction lower, he'd be able to…

She leaned forward even more….

His head followed, and he could almost make out…

"Oh," she muttered, and then snapped up from the chair, regretfully pushing the robe back into place. Her busy hands were back at his jaw, twisting, her brown eyes all business, studying him again.

"Sorry," he said, wondering what she would think if he

pulled her down to the bed for a momentary intermission. A break to stir her creative juices…maybe.

She shook her head. "The look in your eyes. It's wrong. Can we put the sadness back?"

He looked at her in surprise. "Excuse me?"

"I've got you half-sad, but I'm not quite finished with it, and you look, well—" the nervousness was back in her face "—not sad."

"I'm very sorry, but you make me…completely not sad," he said.

That brought her out of her reverie.

"Really?" She looked at him, a pleased smile stretched across her face.

"Really."

"Maybe I shouldn't worry about the sad look. Maybe I could draw you like this," she muttered, looking lower, and then faltering for a second.

Daniel felt his patience coming to an unrepentant, crashing halt, and he was a patient guy, but this was flat-ass weird. "You want the sad back? Keep staring at me like that and stay about four feet away. That's sad."

"Wow," she breathed.

"'Wow' was not the word I would use," Daniel said, fighting the urge to cover himself. Dammit, some things couldn't be helped, and he wasn't going to apologize for it.

Her mouth pulled into another smile, equally pleased as before, but a little bit wicked, and she slid the robe off her shoulders and climbed on top of him. He showed her exactly how "not sad" he felt.

THEY DID EVENTUALLY make it outside. The late-summer sun burned down on her fair skin, the air was sticky, the sand hot, and the water looked too cool to ignore. Daniel was a good swimmer, not as good as she was—she, who had been the breaststroke champion at St. Ignatius, until Mrs. Crawford, the evil school nurse, had told her that swimming made her body look too much like a boy's.

Thank you, Mrs. Crawford.

But Daniel didn't seem to care. He caught her a few times, pulling her under the surface, touching her in ways that told her that he liked her body fine.

Take that, Mrs. Crawford.

Although one thing Catherine did notice was that he was never overt, never committing too much, always watching the lawyers next door with a careful eye. Daniel and Catherine appeared to be two swimmers in the sea, not two lovers lingering on the beach, but she decided that it wasn't going to bother her. After all, she wasn't the demonstrative type, either.

As the afternoon sun moved low they came out of the water. Daniel told her more about himself. He talked about his job at the accounting firm, about his brother's bar. He asked her questions about where she worked, and this time Catherine was the careful one. Normally she loved to talk about Montefiore's, but with all the talk in the back hallways of the auction house, she needed to be extra careful. So she told him she was gainfully employed at an art gallery in Soho where she did appraisals.

Catherine was always cautious.

Daniel listened, asking her polite questions about the business, and she gave her carefully constructed, socially acceptable tales of the canvas, and he didn't seem to notice.

She avoided checking her watch, but eventually the sun started dipping lower in the horizon, and she knew it was close to time. Not wanting him to bring it up first, she glanced pointedly at her watch...once—but it was enough.

He met her eyes, and the loneliness returned. Odysseus was back on his travels. "I should get packed."

Catherine sighed, then stood, dusting off the remains of the sand from her legs. "I'll call you a taxi."

"That'd be good," he said, in a voice best described as emotionless.

This was it. That awkward moment when nothing more is going to come about, but everyone is expected to be adult. Catherine was supposed to pretend she hadn't given her body to a man who was virtually a stranger, yet she'd never felt a stronger connection with a stranger, never felt a stronger connection with a non-stranger, either, for that matter.

Not many men understood a woman like Catherine. She'd spent so much of her life staring at art, studying art and drawing art. She lived in a quiet, inanimate world and at some point, the world became her, and she became the world. And actually, Catherine was happy in that quiet, inanimate world.

Daniel, with his lonely eyes. She'd thought this man understood her, but with every second that passed she felt him putting distance between them. Yes, she wanted to see him again, but she wasn't going to ask, and put herself out there. This was one weekend only. A limited engagement.

Daniel followed her into the house and headed for the bedroom where his things were. The unused bedroom.

After Catherine called the cab, she stood over the kitchen counter. Her hands gripped the cool granite. Some part of her didn't want this to end, but what choice did she have? Eventually, she spotted a bottle of water, helpful for his train ride back to the city, and her genetically propagated social skills came to the rescue.

With the travel refreshment in hand, she went to the bedroom. He didn't notice her at first because he was engrossed in something entirely new and different—the heavy gold band sitting on top of his duffel bag.

*A wedding ring.*

Okay, that explained it. Catherine ignored the shooting pains radiating up from her gut to somewhere near her heart. She did hand him the bottle of water. In times of crisis, always best to remember one's social skills.

She tried to not look at the small circle of gold. However, like the Mona Lisa, it drew your eye like a magnet.

*A wedding ring.*

Not quite what she had imagined.

"It's not what you think," he said, easily reading her mind. Catherine didn't have the patience to hear excuses, not when she suddenly understood why he hadn't cared if she talked much.

Catherine Montefiore, walking vagina. That was her.

"Don't say anything. It's better that way. I'll think more highly of you if you don't try and wangle your way out of this."

Soullessly, he stared at her, and again she felt it, that complete isolation of his, but now it made more sense. It took a cold man to do what he did.

He nodded curtly. "You're right. I'm sorry. I should have told you up front."

"You should have," she replied tightly. Thankfully, she heard a car horn. "What amazing timing. Taxi's here."

He donned his ring, slung the duffel over his shoulder and gave her one last look. "I know you don't want to hear this, but I liked being with you. It's been a long time since I've felt like that. It felt good. You should know that."

Catherine fisted her hands behind her back, her mouth scrunched together. She didn't want to yell. Not yet. Not until he was gone. What an easy mark. For that she hated herself nearly as much as she hated him.

"You're right. I don't want to hear that," she told him, waiting until he walked out the door and left.

After she heard the rev of the taxi pulling away, Catherine

went to take a shower. A long shower because right then she needed nothing more than to get clean.

Sadly, she knew the shower wasn't going to help.

# 5

—————

ON MONDAY DANIEL went back to work at the accounting firm that he'd worked for for the past thirteen years. The Manhattan office of the Big Six firm had once been a bustling, lively place. That changed after 9/11. The office had moved to midtown, before eventually relocating back downtown where it belonged. Daniel was a partner now, but he didn't like the management aspect of accounting. He had found his niche in the accounting world—audits—and that was where he stayed.

The day creaked by slowly. He finished his report on the Hudson Electronics audit, took care of some tax documents, cleared out his in-box, but his conscience wasn't in a good place. His wedding ring was firmly back on his finger, and his life was firmly back where he'd left it on Friday.

Except for the dream last night.

He hadn't been expecting that. That 2:00 a.m. wake-up call when he could feel Catherine next to him, when he could hear her soft voice whispering in his ear. Daniel had woken up with the sheets damp, and his usual raging hard-on, but this time it wasn't Michelle he was reaching for.

He hadn't planned on seeing Catherine again. He purposefully hadn't asked for a phone number because he knew his mind was in no condition to do anything resembling normal.

Still, he hated the aftertaste in his mouth. The taste of accusations unsaid, and the cold, flat look that she leveled him with as he left. This from a woman who didn't do cold or flat well. But she had learned fast.

Yes, it would be easier if Catherine thought he had cheated on his wife. She was better off without him. But Daniel never cheated. Ever. He had been the best husband he could be.

So what did he expect to tell her?

*Oh, yeah, maybe we could go out. Maybe we could sleep together because I really enjoyed that part, but I loved my wife desperately and I don't think I could ever replace her in my heart, and oh, you wouldn't mind if I used you, would you?*

Daniel exhaled and turned back to the tidy world of accounting. There everything came together in the end, debits and credits balanced, for every liability, there was an equal and opposite asset and emotions didn't screw with you at all. He willed himself to concentrate on the numbers, and that self-deception was working nicely until Gabe called him.

"I need your help tomorrow night."

"No," he answered, his eyes burning from lack of sleep, and staring at too much nothing on the screen.

"I haven't asked."

"I'm tired."

"Long weekend?" asked Gabe, heavy innuendo in his voice.

"No," Daniel lied automatically. This weekend was a secret that was going with him to the grave.

"I heard you met somebody."

*So much for secrets. Weren't lawyers supposed to know how to keep their mouth shut?* "We live in New York. If you analyze the population per capita, I have a higher chance of getting hit by lightning than of not meeting somebody."

Gabe laughed, but knew when to quit. "Never mind. I need you to come into the bar tomorrow and work with the new bartender. He's a little slow."

"I'm not a bartender. I'm an accountant. You do it."

"I can't. I'm working on the construction."

"Don't we pay construction people to do that?"

"There's another issue with the building permit. Some official lady-type came in today, saying that we've been designated a historical building."

"It sorta is," Daniel reminded him.

It had been over a year ago when Gabe had bought the space next door to Prime, his goal to restore the old speakeasy to its original size and grandeur. Since then, the problems hadn't stopped. Each time they got one problem solved, a new one popped up. First it was the liquor license, which delayed the building permit, which caused a hiccup in the financing. Then, the steam tunnels running underneath the sidewalk had failed an inspection, and while the repairs were being made, the space sat idle for months. In the spring, the city sent them a bill for nearly six figures of back taxes. It was a computer error, thank God, but now this. Daniel sighed, mainly to make Gabe feel better.

"I don't want my bar to be a freaking historical building on an architectural tour. All I want is to get Prime back to the way it was in the day. Twelve months I've been fighting this. It's like it's cursed. When they gave me the permit in May, I thought it was over. And now I have a wall that's half torn down, a canvas tarp that's trying to cover the hole and somebody's going to catch on to the situation really quick. I'd like to finish this, Daniel. Soon. I'd like to at least finish the demolition on the wall before it starts leaking blood, or they find Jimmy Hoffa's body buried underneath it and it's designated a crime scene."

"What about Sean?" he asked. For Daniel, bartending was the worst sort of torture. He didn't have Gabe or Sean's easy gift for conversation.

"Sean's got a date."

"Tell him to cancel it."

"With the chairman of the city planning department's secretary? She's going to find out what's up with the historical designation."

"What about Cain?" he asked, getting desperate.

"What do you think? He's only part-time. Otherwise he's out fighting fires, Daniel. Don't you think you can spend a night working the place and teaching someone how to bartend?"

Daniel groaned, seeing the hard truth in front of him. He was going to have to bartend. Worse yet, he was going to have to work with some knucklehead who didn't know a whiskey from a water and probably thought all women should be called "baby."

"I'll do it." Now that it was starting to sink in how much his brothers were worrying about him, Daniel wasn't about to let them down. Not anymore.

But that didn't mean he had to like it.

MONTEFIORE Auction House was located at the south edge of Morningside Heights in a squat five-story building that had housed as many art treasures as the Louvre, the Hermitage and MoMA combined, or at least that's what Catherine's grandfather had told her since she was six. Ten years later, when she was an intern there, Catherine realized that perhaps Grandpa might have overexaggerated, but it didn't matter. For her, the storerooms of Montefiore's were as magical as any circus, as spiritual as any cathedral, as addictive as any red velvet cupcake. Well, almost.

Within these boxes and meticulously cataloged crates were the lives, secrets, histories and loves of the world's greatest artists. Men and women whose creations were destined to live forever. She envied them their ability to make the canvas tremble, their sure-handed mastery of color and light, the precisely rendered details that seemed to flow effortlessly. Two hundred, three hundred, four hundred years later, all that was left of their life was the work itself.

*That* was a legacy.

Unfortunately Catherine didn't have her mother's eye for Western contemporary art, nor her grandfather's passion for thirteenth-century Japanese funeral vases, but that didn't stop her from working to develop something that hadn't been passed on in her genes.

For the previous thirteen years, she had learned the business side, studied art history and poured herself into this place. Everything had been okay until she realized that her grandfather had expectations of her outside of the art. At the receptions, she was supposed to be animated, lively. She, who didn't have a vivacious bone in her body. At first, she tried, but then, somewhere along the line, she stopped trying, and accepted who she was, and realized that she couldn't be who her grandfather wanted her to be. She was at peace, but sometimes it hurt.

When the genuine Charles II longcase clock in the lobby chimed nine times, the phones began to ring, and didn't stop until the switchboard operator hit the kill button and everyone breathed a sigh of relief. During the day there were calls from consignors, buyers, art dealers, private appraisers, antique dealers and the relatives who needed a quick appraisal of their parents' artwork that they'd found in the attic.

Maybe Catherine didn't have her grandfather's talent with the public, but she was capable, calm, and had quieted more than her share of anxious consignors.

Today, she preferred the stress to dwelling on the events of the weekend.

*Married.*

Catherine had slept with a married man. Bastard. It was one of those cardinal rules that was so cardinal, she'd never even contemplated the idea that she'd break it.

And why did it have to be so right? Wasn't infidelity sex

supposed to, by its very nature, be sordid and tawdry, not reverent and world-stirring?

Thankfully, the phone rang, and Catherine spent the next hour listening to the Duchess of Marbury's tirade on how her Louis XIV omolu-mounted center table—circa 1685, lest Catherine forget that important detail—had been undervalued at auction. By the time the Duchess had finished, Catherine was ready to forgo art for something less irritable. Like coffee.

Sybil and Brittany met her in the break room. The Monday-morning coffee break was a well-established tradition between the three friends. Although, Catherine wasn't exactly looking forward to it, not after the past couple of days she'd had, but they'd know something was wrong if she didn't show, and married-sex wasn't a crime she was going to confess to. Ever.

"How was the beach?" asked Sybil, pouring her a cup of coffee. "We looked for you on Sunday, but I figured you had chickened out of brunch, and it was, like, so bad you did, because Carol Markowitz was all over Paul Connelly—the slut. I was, like, dying to drag her sorry reputation over the coals, but alas, I was solo, and there was nobody I could whisper catty things to. Men just don't seem to get it. Completely spoiled my good time, I want you to know."

Catherine faked a casual smile. "I wanted some quality downtime. I started this great book. Seemed a waste not to finish it while I had the opportunity."

"Oh. I was hoping it'd be more exciting," said Sybil, who was impatiently waiting for Mr. Right to sweep her off her feet.

"Sorry." Then Catherine noticed Brittany idly staring at the row of auction catalog covers on the wall. When Brittany dodged eye contact, it meant only one thing. Brittany had fallen off the Michael-wagon.

Sybil, never shy, immediately started in. "You saw Michael, didn't you?"

Brittany shrugged one slim shoulder. With black leggings, a black T-shirt, and black thick-rimmed glasses, she could have stepped right out of an art house poetry reading.

Michael was her sometime boyfriend, and full-time jerk, whom Catherine and Sybil had been trying to wean her off of.

"No big deal," answered Brittany, which meant they'd had sex.

Sybil heaved a sigh, tossing back her long fall of auburn hair. "He's never going to respect you if you don't respect yourself. Did he at least call you for a date first?"

"No."

*Of course, Daniel didn't ask Catherine out on a date, either.*

"Did he, like, say anything to indicate you were anything more than a brief bedtime distraction?"

Brittany winced. "No."

Catherine frowned.

*Nothing.* Not a word. And Daniel was married. Michael, at least, was single.

Catherine glanced sympathetically at Brittany, and Sybil spotted it. "Why aren't you backing me up on this?"

Catherine smiled tightly, and Sybil threw up her hands. "Fine. Go ahead, like, desert me when we should be standing together, and see if I forget it, or better yet, if I don't opt to tell you the latest."

Sybil's office was next to the board of directors' meeting room, and she usually got the good board gossip before even Catherine. A bonus to their friendship.

"Don't tell me it's bad." She didn't want bad today. She needed happy, cheerful. Something good. Anything.

"Chadwick's commission structure for the last six months looks remarkably like Montefiore's."

The break room got quiet, deathly quiet, since this was a gazillion times worse than bad. There were three big auction houses in New York. Montefiore, Chadwick and Smithwick-

Whyte. Chadwick's was number two behind Montefiore, their main competitor, and a name usually not spoken, except in a casual, expletive-laden sort of manner.

When two competing firms had the same commission structure, the government got very angry and called it price-fixing, assuming that the two companies were artificially inflating prices. And not only did the government get angry, but the auction house customers weren't happy about it, either. In the upper echelon of the auction business, if your customers were unhappy and didn't trust you, you might as well shut the doors forever.

"That's impossible," Catherine blurted out. "Commission structures are state secret and too variable to be the same." It was true. There were two parts to auction house income. Commissions charged on items to be auctioned and the commission on the sale itself. It was a delicate balancing act and always fluid.

"That's what I heard. The board is completely not happy. It was a customer who brought the matter to their attention. A customer quite capable of starting ugly rumors that the board wanted to quash right away before the government stepped in or before the news got whiff of it." Sybil shrugged, wrinkling a crisp linen dress that had probably cost a fortune. That was why Catherine liked her. She had the money, the class, the style, but she didn't lord it over others, like the debutantes who flocked to Montefiore for jobs.

"I'll talk to Grandpa."

Brittany, much more comfortable telling other people how to live, launched off. "Catherine, think. This could be your chance. You've been looking for a way to impress your grandfather. You should do something. Head it off at the pass. Tell him you'll help, go over the books and show everybody what a crisis they're making of nothing. You'll be the hero. Your grandfather would love it."

Brittany meant well, but Catherine still winced. It'd taken her four years to work her way to art specialist. Nepotism might be alive and well in America, but not at Montefiore. "Maybe we should leave the books to the experts?"

"I think you should try. I bet your grandfather would appreciate the concern."

Catherine met Sybil's eyes and didn't like what she saw there. "I'll talk to him this afternoon," she said, sounding much braver than she felt.

CATHERINE WORKED through lunch, the catering company delivering her usual turkey and Swiss on wheat. While she ate, she silently rehearsed her talk with her grandfather, until she finally found the right mix of firm resolution and cheerful optimism.

She wasn't normally this nervous. She loved her grandfather dearly; however, that didn't change the fact that he was an intimidating figure, albeit not in a bad way, but in a be-all-that-you-can-be way. He was a trailblazer, a renegade, an icon in the art world, and if someone wasn't a trailblazer, didn't have a renegadeish bone in the body, and had yet to master the concept of be-all-that-you-can-be at the ripe old age of twenty-eight—nearly twenty-nine—intimidation was perfectly understandable.

And this was more than asking to borrow the beach house for a weekend. Montefiore's had dodged some scandals in the past—her Gainsborough incident ranked high on the list—but these days the stakes were even higher. Her grandfather had sold off a percentage of the firm to a private equity company in order to finance the opening of London and Paris offices. They both were now profitable, but one financial misstep, and the board would replace Charles Montefiore with someone whose name wasn't Montefiore. In leaner times, people didn't seem to care whose name was on the letterhead. And while other people might not care, she did. Catherine adjusted her jacket, fluffed her hair, squared her shoulders and checked the mirror for the trademark Montefiore gleam in her eye. It didn't happen often, but she could fake it with the best of them.

Once on the top floor, Catherine waved at her grandfather's secretary, who flagged her in. Catherine settled into the old chair until Charles Montefiore got off the phone. According to her grandfather, Winston Churchill had sat in this very chair and written his speeches. The age was right, but the faint aroma of cigars was missing, so Catherine suspected that this was another tale her grandfather had told.

Her grandfather, even seated, towered over most everyone. He was tall, pickwick-lean, with a booming voice that carried perfectly in an auction, and a shock of gray hair that never looked combed. Catherine adored that about her grandfather. In the art world, where customers showed up in four-thousand-dollar dresses, Charles Montefiore had a cowlick that didn't phase him.

He didn't wear glasses, said that they distorted his vision and discolored the world. To prove it he'd always find the misplaced color of a brush stroke, a chip hidden in marble or a counterfeit signature.

After he hung up the phone, those sharp eyes looked at her expectantly.

Catherine tugged at her slacks. "I've heard the rumors," she started inelegantly.

"Forget the speech, Catherine. There's no need for rehearsals. I'm your grandfather, and this isn't the state of the union."

She blushed, but trudged onward. Remember, firm resolution and cheerful optimism. Just like Churchill.

"I think you need to act. Go on the offensive. Kick some board-butt before they can come after you. Think about it, Grandpa, you take the high road, arrange for an audit, and then—"

He held up a hand, stopping her midspeech. "I've already told them to go ahead with the audit."

"Well," Catherine said, blowing out a breath. "That's good. An audit will prove that we didn't do anything wrong and our customers can again have complete faith in us. And that the board was wrong to doubt you for a moment. Excellent plan." Thinking of the best way to charge forward and telling him that she wanted to help was much more difficult than cheerful optimism.

"You might need some help," she said, not quite blazing forward, but hinting broadly nonetheless.

"I put Foster Sykes in charge. He's making the call this afternoon. He'll pull all the invoices from the sales and let the numbers speak for themselves." Foster was the accounting VP. Capable, intelligent, good at his job and never fooled by a fake Gainsborough in his life.

"Oh," answered Catherine weakly.

"Did you want to add something?" he asked, noting her carefully from under bushy, silvered brows.

"If you do need some help—"

"Speak up, girl!"

"I could do it," she finished, much more firmly. Much more firmly. Definitely.

"Are you sure about that? High dollars and math. Not quite your thing."

"No, it isn't," she said, staring dubiously at her notes.

"Then how could you help?"

Finance. Dollars. Math. All areas where she could contribute absolutely nothing. "Never mind," said Catherine, stuffing her hands deeply into her pockets. Maybe next time.

"You're not going to help?"

"I probably shouldn't," she muttered.

"That's all you wanted?" he asked.

"That's it," she said, smoothing her hair with her hand.

"Too bad," he answered. "Get back to work, then." Catherine hurried out the door, but felt his eyes on her, watching. Watching her with disappointment.

*Well, that makes two of us, doesn't it.*

# 6

———

IT WAS A HOT Tuesday night, and Prime was unseasonably slow. Thankfully.

Lloyd, Syd and E.C. were sitting behind the bar. They were a motley crew of old-timers who had been coming to Prime since Daniel had been a kid watching his uncle tend bar.

Lloyd had been an ironworker for most of his life, and had the ruddy complexion to prove it—and the bronchitis, as well. E.C. had been an engineer for MTA, but you'd never know it by talking to him. He talked like a professor, carried his tall frame like a professor and had two ex-wives, who wished he'd been paid like a professor. Syd was one of New York's finest, who, at fifty-one, planned on working past his retirement age because the force and the bar were about all he knew.

Behind the long mahogany bar at the back of the place, Tessa was working, a tiny figure with a really cocky mouth, and Daniel was happily surprised to see her. Although she'd been a great bartender at Prime, she'd quit in order to pursue a bigger, better and more financially stable future in the real estate biz— and also to move in with his brother.

"Where's Gabe?" he asked, and Tessa pointed behind the green tarp that covered one half of a wall. "Follow the sound of drilling, punctuated by assorted obscenities. There, you'll find your brother."

The music was turned up on high, but even the sounds of

the Red Hot Chili Peppers couldn't drown out the steady whir. Then the drilling stopped, Tessa held up a wait-for-it finger and immediately the sound of pain split through the bar, followed by a word that their mother, Katie O'Sullivan, had never let them utter without dire consequences. Their father, Thomas O'Sullivan, had never taken to the bar, choosing to work for a newspaper instead, and left Uncle Patrick to run the bar. Thomas had passed away while Daniel was in high school; his brother Patrick had passed away ten years later. There were only three remaining O'Sullivans now. Daniel, Gabe and Sean. Daniel's eyes automatically went to the framed picture of their mother and their uncle standing behind the bar. The walls were full of pictures from the establishment over the years. It was the history of the bar consolidated in five-by-seven images.

When their great-grandfather had first started O'Sullivan's, it was a speakeasy serving politicians and robber barons. Over the years, the clientele changed. The bar served gin to Mafia dons, Yankee sluggers and even two presidents. For every moment in the bar's history, there was a photograph to prove it.

"Where's the new guy?" Daniel asked, hoping the employee was a no-show.

"Bringing up beer," Tessa answered with a satisfied smile. "I see a strong man. I put him to work. I've conquered independence, now I'm moving on to delegation. And here's my faithful minion now." She cocked her head toward the male emerging via the basement stairs.

"What's next, ma'am?" the new bartender asked dutifully.

Tessa beamed. "He's so obedient. Daniel, this is Jackson."

Jackson looked barely legal, but he had some meat on him and kept grinning nervously every time Tessa said his name.

Daniel held out his hand. "Daniel O'Sullivan."

Jackson stared at Daniel's hand and then tapped his fist to

it. From the front side of the bar, E.C. howled with laughter, and Daniel understood why. There was probably fourteen years of age separating Daniel from Jackson, but God help him, now it felt like fourteen hundred.

Desperately, Daniel looked at Tessa. "You're here. I could leave, couldn't I?"

Tessa shook her head. "Nope. You're stuck here till closing."

Daniel remembered his new resolution to make his brothers happy, and didn't scowl at Jackson, but it was difficult. "All right. Two rules. Tessa will tell you what to do and you call any woman 'honey' or 'baby' and you're fired."

"He's always like this," Tessa said, feeling the need to explain things to Jackson. Daniel faked a smile.

"That's true," added Lloyd.

"Where's Charlie?" Daniel asked, proud of himself for managing friendly conversation. It was like riding a bicycle. He hadn't forgotten, he was merely out of practice. He looked over at Tessa, but regretfully she hadn't even noticed. Jackson, however, was still grinning broadly.

"Sad," answered Syd.

Daniel looked at him with concern. "The new guy?"

"No, Charlie, He's wandered wide-eyed into matrimonial bliss," answered E.C., who didn't seem to bear any scars from his divorces.

"Sad," Syd repeated, shaking his dark head. As far as Daniel knew, Syd had never been married, always alone, a man of habits, none of them good.

"A toast to the new bride and groom," Lloyd said, lifting his glass, and four sets of eyes stared at Daniel expectantly.

"What?" he said, feeling something twitchy behind his neck.

"Aren't you going to give us a round on the house?" E.C. asked, as if free drinks were a constitutional right. "To celebrate the nuptials of a man who's been a customer here for over fifty years. It's tradition." He looked pointedly at Jackson. "You have to train the bartenders correctly from day one."

Daniel wavered because this was a tough one. The price of alcohol had shot up twenty-seven percent over the past three years, and he didn't want to free-drink the bar into bankruptcy, but they were talking about marriage. Jackson looked at Daniel, waiting.

No one understood the cost of things. Everyone moved blithely through life without once thinking of the consequences. Every decision, every transaction, had consequences.

He frowned, and Syd glared at Tessa. "Did you have to put the accountant behind the bar?"

Tessa shrugged. "Sorry. He's part owner."

Oh, fine. "What do you want?" Daniel asked, and then started making drinks.

"Sorry," said Daniel, who looked expectantly at Jackson. "You're training here. Help out." Then he turned to Tessa. "I should give him more responsibility, don't you think? I could go downstairs, finish up with the payroll."

Tessa stopped him with a deceptively strong hand to the arm. "No."

He looked at her, defeat in his eyes. "I had to try."

"You should listen more to Gabe. And Sean," she added reluctantly.

Oh, he knew where this was leading. "Let's talk about something else, okay? How's the career coming?" Daniel smiled to himself, happy with the neat conversation change.

At that, her eyes lit up. Tessa loved talking real estate. "Oh, yeah, tell me about the house! You got a chance to look at the one I asked you to, right? I'm looking for something classically Greek, but with a comfortable feel to it. It's for an older couple. Not retired, but thinking about more long summers away from the city. Was the lighting good? They need good lighting. Too dark and a place gets dreary."

*Damn*. Daniel had forgotten about that bit of responsibility this weekend. If he admitted to not seeing it, he'd have to share an explanation of why he hadn't fulfilled his responsibility. He, who always fulfilled his responsibilities.

"I hated it," he said, not meeting her eyes.

"Too dark?"

"Definitely," he lied.

"What about the view?"

"The view?"

"Yeah, the pictures from the file looked like a postcard, but you can't really trust that. I mean, are you looking out their window, or the neighbor's window, or is it a zoom lens from two miles down the road? People lie."

"I didn't notice the view," he said, shamed into honesty.

"Oh." She studied him suspiciously. Tessa knew that Daniel wouldn't miss anything.

"It was late when I drove past it," he said, hoping that'd be enough.

"Okay." They were blessedly interrupted when a man came up to the bar and ordered a rum and Coke from Jackson, who looked at Tessa helplessly.

"You should tell him what's in it," encouraged Daniel, now trying to be helpful, since it got him out of the weekend conversation.

"Gabe said you met somebody." She burst his bubble, all the while pouring the drinks. That was Tessa. Multitasking was her specialty.

"Nope," he lied again, wondering what had happened to his ethics, his scruples, his moral conscience. But the idea of his family staring, asking questions, prying into something that he would never repeat anyway… "Read a book. A great thriller."

"Good," she said, and he knew she didn't believe him. He'd never been a good liar, didn't have a deceptive bone in his body.

He was saved from further cross-examination by Gabe bursting out from behind the tarp, holding up something tiny. "Look what I found in the wall."

Daniel moved closer to see. The something was a ring. A diamond ring. An expensive diamond ring. "In the wall?"

Gabe nodded. "It was stuck in the old newspaper insulation. Newspapers. Can you believe it? It's no wonder this place sucks heat in the winter."

"The ring," Tessa reminded him, peeking over Jackson's shoulder.

"It's an engagement ring," commented Lloyd. "Probably from the fifties, by the look of it. My sister got one like it. What a complete waste of money, but then the dolt she married wasn't smart enough to know."

Gabe turned it over in his hand. "There're some markings on the inside. Can't read them."

Tessa took the ring between her fingers and peered at the inside. "I bet it's stolen. I can't see anyone burying it in the wall unless there's a body attached."

"No body," said Gabe. "I checked."

Syd took a look, dark eyes checking out the inscription. "If it was stolen, they should have fenced it. Gotta say that criminals are getting stupider every day." He handed the ring to Daniel. "Can you read that?"

Daniel looked carefully at the dainty ring and the engraving on the inside. Fine print was his specialty. "Forever. B.T.K. S.C.H."

"How sad," murmured Tessa. "Can you imagine having your engagement ring stolen? I hope he bought her a new one."

"If he loved her, he would," said Daniel, holding the ring up to the light. "It's a nice ring. You should find the owner."

"You should keep it," Syd said. "Technically, we don't know if it's stolen property. Legally, it belongs to the owner of the property it's found on. That's Gabe."

Gabe reached for it, but Daniel held on to the ring. "What if someone's still looking for this?"

"After sixty years?" Gabe asked.

"We don't know that for certain." Daniel was ready to put his brother back in his place. "What if it's only been six months or even six years? That's not long enough for people to quit looking. If it was me, I'd look forever. A ring can't be replaced. A man agonizes over finding the exact ring that's worthy of the only woman that he'll ever love. It's a symbol to the world that this one woman belongs to him and she'll be first in everything that he does. It's a lot more than just a ring."

Gabe looked over at Tessa, eyes considering.

"Don't look at me like that," she warned.

However, Daniel knew what his baby brother was like. Tessa was sunk. Daniel smiled.

"I think Daniel's right," Gabe said stubbornly.

"Daniel's being a schmuck," said Syd. "Keep the damn thing. Nobody will turn up."

Gabe was now fully engaged, and he laid the ring on the counter, all eyes staring at it. "What if there're two lovers out there somewhere, and she's thinking that he doesn't love her enough to give her a ring, or he's thinking that she threw the ring in the garbage, and they're never going to be together because of that ring?"

"You should find the owners. It's the right thing to do." Daniel didn't like the idea of someone out there lost without their ring. To remind himself of exactly how lucky he'd been, he tapped his own band.

Gabe handed him the ring. "Okay. We'll do it. But since I have a bar that's currently fronting as an open-air café, it's your job."

Daniel frowned, pocketing the ring. No one understood that true love wasn't replaceable or forgotten. True love was forever. But Daniel understood.

He'd loved Michelle, and it was forever.

He felt more settled inside, easing some of the guilt from this weekend. He'd had a fling, a chance to burn off some tension, but that was done.

"So, let's show this kid how to bartend," he said, taking a deep breath.

CATHERINE KNEW the tense situation at Montefiore Auction House was serious when her mother flew in from the London office. Andrea Montefiore had never missed the run-up to the fall British auction season, not once in the past seven years. She was the world's premier expert on English furniture, and no surprise, the best pieces came out of Montefiore's London branch, where she was in charge.

In mid-August, auctions were being scheduled, deliveries and contracts were being signed, catalogs were being photographed and, in general, it was no time for Andrea Montefiore to leave her post.

The situations was dire at Montefiore's.

People talked in whispers, and even Sybil had nothing to share.

Over dinner some nights, Catherine would try to get her mother to tell her what she knew, but Andrea Montefiore was as clueless as everyone else.

The only upside to the Montefiore crisis was that Catherine had nearly put that one infamous weekend out of her mind. *Almost.*

Sometimes she thought about him. She nearly used Google to find him twice. Even her normally tidy studio apartment was littered with sketches. Catherine would sketch a picture, gaze in awe, and then, mad at herself for obsessing over him, would scribble darkly until the whole image was unsalvageable. Sadly, artistic exorcism wasn't working.

The autumn showers started, rain hammering late in the

afternoon, and it was on one such foul day when the hammer came down.

The board suspected not just any employee—oh, no—but Charles Montefiore himself, of collusion with Chadwick's.

Andrea Montefiore delivered the news in person. She seemed calm, poised, elegant and completely in control. Except for the unlit cigarette dangling from her mother's fingers, Catherine would have assumed everything was fine. Andrea had quit smoking twelve years ago.

Catherine's relationship with her mother was more complicated than most, although to be fair, she wasn't sure if there was such a thing as an uncomplicated mother-daughter relationship. She and her mother shared a passion for good art, good knockoff purses and, when her mother had smoked and could afford the extra calories, a passion for buttercream cupcakes, as well.

However, the two areas in which Catherine surpassed her mother—knockoff purses and buttercream cupcakes—weren't the two she would have chosen for herself if she'd been dipping in to the talent pool.

So, while Catherine had a closetful of faux designer bags and size-six jeans that her mother had given to her and Catherine couldn't wear, but wouldn't admit to, her mother had a closetful of Armani and size-four jeans and a secret carton of Virginia Slims that Catherine knew she kept in case of emergency.

No matter her minor transgressions, Catherine loved her mother, and it pained her to see the tight lines around her mother's mouth.

"The board ordered an independent audit. They're coming in today and will report to the board in two weeks' time. We're to cooperate fully," her mother explained, speaking in the cultured tones that came from an Oxford education.

"Grandpa didn't do anything."

"Of course not, but it's best to let this run its course, and then we'll simply laugh over the silly matter when it's done."

The unlit cigarette flipped awkwardly between her mother's lips.

Catherine leaned forward, kissed her on the cheek and removed the cigarette from her mother's mouth.

"I wasn't going to light it," Andrea said defensively.

Catherine smiled at her soothingly. "I know," she answered, but she broke it in half and threw it in the trash anyway. "Have you talked to Grandfather? Should I talk to him?"

Andrea patted her hand. "No, dear. There are four crates coming in from Cairo, and I'd feel better if you'd make sure the transit documents are complete. You'll do it, won't you?"

And so Catherine was sent to the docks to help inventory the shipment. She took an assistant and a driver, and they made it there without incident, but coming back, the rain began to fall in great sheets. At Montefiore's, Catherine stepped from the vehicle onto the sidewalk and hit a tidal wave of swirling water. Her dress was soaked, her hair was soaked, her whole body was a sticky, soggy mess. Shaking out her umbrella, she walked into the grand lobby of the building as the clock struck six.

The elevator dinged, and she tapped the umbrella impatiently on the marble floor, anxious to get into something dry. The doors opened, and just as the huddle of men moved to exit, she saw him. There in the back.

Daniel O'Sullivan.

In the flesh.

# 7

CATHERINE STOOD ASIDE, letting the group pass, Charles Montefiore in the lead. Foster Sykes, head of accounting, was at his elbow. And behind them—

*The bastard.*

She was going to ignore him, she was going to let him walk right past her, and pretend that he'd never occupied even one second of her life, and it worked well. Until she got into the elevator, turned around and met his eyes.

Oh, *no.*

His eyes flared with something more than recognition and he practically jumped away from the group. "I think I left my phone upstairs. Excuse me," he said, neatly sliding into the elevator beside her.

He was dressed in a dark suit. Conservative blue tie, crisp white shirt and an American flag tie-tack.

Catherine looked away, acting as if he wasn't there, but she could smell the sandalwood cologne and knew.

Was she ever going to forget that smell? Would her body ever stop arching toward it?

She tried to call up all the anger, shame and regret that she had buried inside her. Everything she had to keep from falling for the exquisite sadness in his face.

"Catherine."

"Don't talk to me," she snapped, her eyes focused on the

tight weave of the Savonnerie rug that covered the elevator floor. It had been designed for Louis XIV, circa 1712, and had a value of over fifty thousand dollars. Her dress and coat were dripping all over it.

*Probably ruining it.*

"You need to listen."

She could hear the dings as the floors ticked past, and the old elevator lumbered up interminably slow.

Two.

Three.

"Please," he said.

"No, I don't think there's anything to say."

"I should have told you."

"Yes. You should. I never would have…would have…if you had."

"That's not what I'm trying to say."

Four.

Her hand clenched around the carved wooden handle of her umbrella, tighter, squeezing it as if it were alive. "I don't want to listen. I've never done anything like that in my life, and now I'm going to have to live with it."

Five.

The elevator dinged, and his hand reached out, grabbed her. His left hand. The one with the ring.

She pulled away as the doors opened.

"Catherine. I'm widowed."

AS SOON AS HE said the words, Daniel felt something burst inside him. He didn't say them often. He didn't like the way they sounded, or the way people looked at him after they knew.

The way Catherine was looking at him now. She stuck her umbrella into the elevator, stepped back inside and watched him with wide brown eyes that were wary—but not angry, not anymore. Thank God.

"You're telling me the truth?" she asked.

Automatically the elevator doors shut and the car descended. Daniel desperately wanted to talk to her, he needed to talk to her, but he wouldn't talk here. There were too many people buzzing around, her coworkers, the people that he'd been working with, as well. It was important for him to appear distant and unbiased with everyone at the auction house. In his profession, appearances were key. "Please, let me explain. Not here."

She was wearing a shell-shocked look; her hair, darkened with the rain, was matted to her head. And she clutched her umbrella like a lifeline. "There's a park next door," she managed finally.

"It's raining."

"There's a gazebo. In the center."

He nodded, and took her umbrella as they headed to the lobby.

The clients from the auction house were gone. Daniel guessed they would be waiting for him at the restaurant. They would survive. He needed to make things right with Catherine.

"You work at Montefiore?"

"My grandfather is Charles Montefiore."

*And wouldn't that be awkward?* Daniel investigating her own blood relation for a potentially criminal offense.

Once outside, the rain was still pelting down, and her opened her umbrella. It wasn't much protection, but he didn't really think it mattered. Holding her arm in his free hand, they crossed Amsterdam Avenue to the park. He spotted the old-fashioned gazebo a few yards ahead. Catherine was still soaked to the skin, but he didn't think she realized it anymore.

She hadn't said another word, and he could feel her shivering. His first instinct was to draw her closer, but that wouldn't be right, and Daniel didn't want to screw things up even more than they already were.

As soon as they were under the gazebo, he leaned the dripping umbrella against the railing, stepping a good distance away. He had no excuse to touch her anymore, so he released her arm. "I'm sorry. I should have said something."

She pushed back the hair from her eyes, her mouth twisted in an awkward imitation of a smile. "Please don't. I've been thinking some very awful things, and—yes, you should have said something."

Daniel stuffed his hands in his pockets, and began to pace around the small space. "Catherine," he stated, and she sat down on the bench, looking up at him nervously.

And now what was he supposed to say? Everything running through his mind sounded wrong, or crude or trite. "I don't know what to say."

Her awkward smile disappeared, leaving no smile, awkward or otherwise, in its place. "I wondered why you were so lonely."

"I wanted to be left alone."

Her head jerked back. "I didn't know. I'm sorry," she said, and he could see the hurt in her face. Way to go, Daniel. Go ahead, shoot Bambi. Kill the puppy. Trample all over the feelings of the first woman you've wanted to be with since…well, since a very long time.

He took an impulsive step toward her, then took a wiser step back. "Not you. You were nice."

"Nice," she repeated to herself, although it sounded more like a curse.

They would both be better off if he just left, disappeared back into the empty hole that he'd crawled out of, but Daniel couldn't. He'd tasted the air above the surface again and it felt too good. "I don't do that. Ever."

She watched him, her eyes judging, assessing, and he wondered what she saw, what she thought, what she felt. But the brown eyes weren't warm and welcoming; the Closed sign was firmly in place.

"When did your wife die?"

He winced, then sat on the bench beside her. "September eleventh."

CATHERINE WITHERED inside. This wasn't cancer. This wasn't a brain tumor. Not even a car accident. What was she supposed to say? The rain pounded down even harder, nearly drowning out the noise inside her head.

Thankfully, he started talking again. His voice was low, even, and she had to lean forward to hear him. "We worked together on the hundred and fourth floor of the North Tower. She had an early meeting to get ready for, so I went to get the coffee. She insisted on this one Starbucks up north on Hudson. Michelle was like that, finding her favorite spot, and not settling for anything less, and I didn't mind. But that morning, the shop was crowded, and there was a kid behind the counter. His name was Marco and I was telling him about the Yankees' chances against the Red Sox, but he was a Mets fan and he wanted to argue, so we sat there shooting the shit, and that's when I heard the boom. I was fourteen blocks away."

Full stop. End of story, and her mind drifted back in time. She had been safe, sitting in a classroom uptown at Columbia. She didn't know anyone who worked in the towers. That wasn't her world. Within the restricted confines and the idealism of the university, she might as well have been in Kansas, except for the black cloud that hung in the sky, and the awful smells that drifted on the air when the wind shifted from the south.

Catherine wanted to look away from him, anywhere, but here she was, helplessly trapped in a nightmare that had started seven years ago. She didn't handle nightmares well; she wasn't one of those women who ran into burning buildings or walked down into dark basements. There were people who were brave and fearless in the face of pain and suffering and then there were people who withdrew even further into their shell—like Catherine.

"I'm sorry." Possibly the two most pathetic words in the world.

"I am, too," he told her, and the distance between them yawned infinitely. Ten feet at most, but a thousand lifetimes away. He rubbed his hands on his pants, and she could see his gaze tracking the path of his ring. And it would be a foolish woman to misunderstand his words.

She wanted to ask about his wife. She would bet that she was pretty and vivacious, the kind of woman that a man didn't forget. Ever. But those sorts of questions would seem petty and impertinent.

He nodded once, a dismissive gesture. "I should go now. I'm supposed to meet your grandfather and Sykes for dinner."

"I won't hold you up," she told him.

Daniel looked at her for a long moment. She knew he was going to say something but she didn't want him to say anything. She wanted to leave that one weekend alone. Buried in a place where they wouldn't have to touch it anymore. So she interrupted him before he could start. "We can forget this. Forget anything happened. It was a while ago."

"Fifteen days," he answered.

She lifted her head and met his eyes with intent. "I've already forgotten."

"I haven't."

Wasn't he supposed to be making this easier on her? She was doing her damnedest to ease him out of this, because she knew, absolutely knew that she'd end up falling in love with this man, and his wife, his beautiful dead wife was going to be forever remembered in monuments and buildings and memorials and scholarships. Maybe Daniel wanted to start over, maybe Daniel didn't, but the city of New York would never let him move past Michelle O'Sullivan.

"Was she pretty?" Catherine asked, a subtle reminder to him of what he lost, a subtle reminder to her of what she couldn't have.

At that, the urgency in his eyes dimmed. "Yeah."

"I'll go now," she said, retrieving the umbrella. It was past time to run.

"Catherine…" he started, and she interrupted because she didn't want to hear this. He was going to say something to make her feel better, because he was that sort of man. He would promise her the world if it would help her, and he'd try really, really hard to keep those promises, but he wouldn't be able to, and Catherine would hurt even worse.

"Please don't."

He nodded. "There's something you should know though. The audit. I'll be working here for the next few weeks."

Catherine had known that. She had realized the implications the minute she saw him in the elevator. But the idea of seeing him every day, nine to five…

It would have been easier if he'd been a married jackass, fooling around on his wife. Now he was only a very nice man with lonely eyes.

Her Odysseus, always looking toward home.

"I can pull myself from the assignment, Catherine."

She stood frozen, standing there under the gazebo, holding her umbrella like an idiot. "You're good at what you do, aren't you?"

"Yeah," he replied, and she knew he would be. He was perfect at everything he did.

Accounting. Making love.

*Mourning.*

"Stay," she told him. "Clear my grandfather."

"He could be involved. He could be in serious trouble."

Catherine shook her head. Some things in the world she wouldn't doubt. Her grandfather was one. "No. You don't know him."

"As an auditor, I can't be seen fraternizing with you personally, only dealing with you professionally. They have rules necessary to maintain the integrity and unbiased nature of the audit. If there's any doubts about it, they'll throw all the work out and start over with someone new. It's not me being rude."

"We've worked with auditors before. Not like this, but I know the drill. No worries here. It'll only make things easier, won't it?"

"I'm sorry," he apologized again.

Catherine managed a polite smile and left.

DANIEL HAD WATER for dinner and not much else. He listened politely as Foster Sykes told a golf story and laughed at the appropriate parts. People handled trouble differently. Some broke down. Some pretended nothing was wrong. And some people looked at him as if he'd stuck a knife between their ribs.

He should have felt relieved after talking to Catherine, but instead all he felt was crap. As he listened purposely to the banter that was a prerequisite for making nice with the client, Daniel ran through all the different ways he could have told her that he couldn't see her because it wouldn't be fair.

But she'd beat him to it.

If this hadn't been a business dinner, he would have ordered a double Jack, straight up, but he was too much of a professional to stay anything other than stone-cold sober.

He could only sit and listen to Charles Montefiore, who had the same owlishly brown eyes as his granddaughter.

*And what if the man was fixing the commissions?*

In any business, talking to your competitors and conspiring to set prices artificially high was illegal. It didn't matter if you kept the price of commissions artifically high for one item or ten million items. It didn't matter if you lined your pockets with an extra ten million dollars in profit, or an extra one dollar in profit. It was illegal, it was irresponsible, and not only could Charles Montefiore go to jail, but it would take years for the auction house to repair its reputation with its customers.

Just one more knife that Daniel could stab his granddaughter with.

Foster cracked another joke, Daniel pretended to laugh and when the server approached again, Daniel ordered a double Jack.

*Screw it.*

CATHERINE OVERSLEPT the next morning because she had spent the night in front of her computer reading all the moving tributes about the late Michelle Mitchell O'Sullivan. She even found their wedding announcement and read that the bride wore a Vera Wang wedding gown, and the reception had been held at a bar on the West Side.

When Catherine dressed for work, she picked her nicest Badgley Mischka black chiffon dress, which didn't compare to a Vera Wang bridal gown. But after she stared at herself in the morning, she thought she'd pass.

Not that anyone would be looking.

Sybil and Brittany were in the break room, whispering over coffee, when she walked in.

"Look at you!" Sybil exclaimed. "You must have seen him, I take it?"

"Who?" Catherine asked, pretending ignorance.

"The guy from MBRC, the accounting firm. I think I'm in love."

Brittany shook her head. "Not me. Definite lust. He's got a ring."

"You're both being ridiculous," Catherine said with a faux grin, as if she hadn't spent the night finding out every possible detail of his life.

"I heard he's not married."

"Then why the ring?" replied Brittany.

"He's widowed," pronounced Sybil, as if this were some state to be desired.

"Oh." Then Brittany made a face. "Did you ask?"

"I heard one of the board members," Sybil answered. "If the guy needs help getting over her, I'm available. This place doesn't provide many opportunities for meeting new men, and I can feel my ovaries hardening."

"Don't be crude," snapped Catherine.

"What's up with you?" asked Brittany, because Catherine was never rude. Ever.

"I'm sorry. I didn't sleep well." And she hadn't. She dreamed most of the night, clutching her pillow as if it had the world's most perfect shoulders, and smelling sandalwood cologne in her sleep. "I'll go," she said. Inside she felt raw and queasy and her mind wasn't able to focus on anything at all.

"Oh, we're only kidding," said Sybil. "I'll behave if I have to. But only if I have to."

"I actually have work to do. Don't tell anybody," Catherine offered with a weak smile. Then she disappeared.

The e-mail was waiting for her when she came back to her computer.

*Come to dinner with me.*

Quietly, Catherine rose, closed her door and laid her head down on the desk. Daniel wanted her, he wanted to sleep with her—until he was ready to move on with his life. Catherine would be his transitional person before he found someone new.

Or even worse, she would be his transitional person, and he would never find any woman that matched up to the memory of his wife.

Could Catherine do that, be that transitional person?

No, but she wasn't strong enough to say no, either.

She took a deep breath, and smoothed the black dress over her thighs because she was about to make the biggest mistake of her life, and she wanted to look nice.

*Yes,* she typed, and then waited impatiently until she got the reply.

One short line of text.

*Bella Cucchina. 7:30.*

AT LUNCHTIME Catherine noticed the boxes of documents being carted up to five—her grandfather's floor. That was where Daniel was. But she didn't go near him. Her stomach was already cramping up with nerves, and then her mother called thirty minutes later asking her to dinner.

"Sorry, Mother," she said, declining gracefully. "I've got some work to do."

It was after seven when she closed and locked her office door. There was a reception that night, a preview showing of the highlights of the fall season, but she could duck out without anyone missing her. Concealer worked miracles to cover the dark circles under her eyes. Her hands shook as she applied the lipstick, and she kept telling herself that she was being silly. It was dinner. Nothing more than that.

But the warning bells inside her clanged with ear-splitting intensity—not that she listened.

# 8

DANIEL'S CELL VIBRATED in his pocket and he answered the call. It was Gabe. A pissy Gabe, but Daniel had expected that.

"I got your message. What does that mean, 'I'm going to miss the poker game'?"

The poker game was a regular Wednesday-night event. Gabe, Daniel, Sean and Cain had played every Wednesday since…pretty much forever. "I thought it was very clear. I'm going to miss the poker game tonight."

"Is this some big accounting job? Because this is family. This is important. Where are your priorities?"

Idly, Daniel stared at the gold band on his finger. He couldn't wear his wedding ring tonight. It was rude to wear a wedding ring to a date. He pulled it off, tried it on his right hand, but it didn't fit. He couldn't wear his ring. He'd have to keep it in his pocket.

"You're only after my money," Daniel answered, frowning.

"Well, it's not your scintillating conversation, in case that's where you've been making your mistake."

"I'll be there next week. Swear."

"Why not tonight?"

"I've got a new assignment for work. It's keeping me busy," said Daniel, thumbing through the last two years' worth of Montefiore's financial statements. Who knew there was this much money in old furniture?

"Claudia called the bar last night looking for you. She said she'd left you a message at your apartment and on your cell, but you hadn't called. She was worried."

Daniel swore under his breath and put the documents aside. Claudia was his mother-in-law. And unlike the other ninety-nine percent of married America, Daniel's mother-in-law was a sweetheart—so much like her daughter that sometimes it hurt. Normally that wasn't a problem. Daniel expected the hurt. And he would have rushed to return the phone call, but something about hearing Claudia's motherly tones made him antsy.

For the last couple of weeks—since *the* weekend in the Hamptons—he'd avoided calling because he thought she'd be able to hear the shift in his voice, not quite so forlorn, not nearly as sad.

"I was telling Sean that I thought you'd gone drinking, but it's getting harder to keep quiet, you know? If you need to sit in a bar and get shitfaced, why don't you come to Prime? At least I'll know you're okay, and don't have to play these guessing games about where I'll need to rescue my brother next."

The knife was twisting, but not in the way Gabe thought. Any other time, Gabe would be exactly right. When it was Michelle's birthday, or their wedding anniversary, or almost any day in September, Daniel would spend his nights out drinking. Sitting alone on an uncomfortable bar stool, chasing whiskey with whiskey because he didn't want to be at home by himself.

However, Daniel hadn't done much late-night drinking lately. Lately, he'd been locked in his apartment, having the most vivid, erotic dreams of his life. And absolutely none that involved his wife.

"I'll call Claudia now," he said.

"I know sometimes you want to be alone—"

*Less than you think.*

"But we're here, too. If you need to talk."

"Sure thing," Daniel said in his happiest, most guilt-free voice. "Have you had any luck on the ring we found in the wall?"

"Not yet. I've searched some archives in the *Times* for those initials, but nothing turned up."

"You should talk to a jewelry appraiser and see if they can tell you anything about it."

"Why so much interest in the ring now, Gabe? Weren't you the one who wanted to keep it?"

"I never said that," his brother answered defensively.

"You were thinking it."

"If it's not spoken aloud, it doesn't count."

"God knows. He knows all." That was why Daniel went to confession once a week, every week. He wanted God—and Michelle—to know that he knew he had broken his wedding vows and messed up.

"Can you keep it shut?" snapped Gabe, who hadn't been to confession since he was sixteen. "I'm doing the right thing now. Find an appraiser and see what they can tell you about it. There's got to be jewelry historian people."

And conveniently, Montefiore must have someone he could hire. "I know just the place," assured Daniel.

"But you're still going to miss the poker game tonight?"

"You'll survive."

"Probably, but Tessa makes me feel guilty about taking money from Sean. She says he's too easy of a mark."

"She only says that because he never put Preparation H in her jockstrap."

"I told her that. It meant nothing."

"Women."

Gabe hesitated. "You're okay? September starts a week from Wednesday."

Daniel looked at the date on his watch. He'd almost lost track. Almost. "Can you stop worrying about me?"

"If you'd do something normal, then I'd stop worrying. I'd think, yeah, he's okay. But you don't. You have two modes—

work-drink or drink-work or work-work-work-drink or dead silence."

"That's four modes," Daniel clarified, because, after all, he did work with numbers for a living. "I have to call Claudia."

"All right, but if you need anything—"

"Bye," Daniel said and quickly hung up.

The next phone call was easier than he thought. Claudia's answering machine kicked in, and he left her a message. The dutiful son-in-law checking in.

After he disconnected, he looked at his watch. Seven-eighteen.

It was too late to turn back now.

Way too late.


THE OFFICE BUILDING that housed Bella Cucchina was all steel and glass, but once you got past the deserted lobby, it was like entering a new world. The tiny Italian bistro had old wooden chairs, waiters with thick, authentic accents, a bottomless bottle of Chianti and Daniel.

Catherine hadn't intended to drink during dinner, but the conversation was slow and awkward, and Daniel was even more withdrawn than yesterday. If she were chatty and bubbly and vivacious, she probably wouldn't have been so self-conscious, but Catherine could never think of things to say, or little bon mots to toss out like sparkling confetti.... Still, Daniel didn't seem to mind.

He would watch her with this look in his eyes. She didn't think he knew, his gaze dark, hungry and raw, moving over her in quicksilver bursts. Between that and the wine, Catherine tried to uncoil...better able to walk through the fire.

He wore the same suit he'd worn at the office, but somewhere he'd ditched the jacket, and she regretted that he'd taken it off. When he was in a suit, all covered and tidy, he was a different man from the one she'd met on the beach. The man she'd sketched, the man she'd made love to.

His left hand was bare, a white strip of skin visible where his ring usually rested. Right now it was probably sitting at his bedside, ready to be put back on when he got home.

"The wine is very good," she said, watching him over the rim of her glass.

"Good. When it comes to wine, I have no idea what I'm doing."

Like art, Montefiore auctioned wines, as well, and Catherine had been to wine tastings and wine classes and knew more than most. "But you do know some. You wouldn't have chosen a 1997 Sangiovese otherwise."

"Must have been a lucky guess," he commented with a shrug.

"I don't think so. I mean, you *do* own a bar." That stopped her. "Tell me again why you own a bar? Everything else makes sense about you, but not that."

"Family obligations more than anything."

"Are your parents still alive?"

"No, my mother died after…recently, and my father died when I was in high school. He was never interested in the bar, left my uncle to run the place, while Dad worked as a reporter for the *Sun*."

"Did you work there growing up?"

"Some. We all did, but it wasn't my thing. I'm not meant to be around people like my brothers were. They were happy. I spent a lot time in the basement doing the dishes. I'm a really good dishwasher."

"I was the cook," she told him, and for a moment they looked at each other silently across the table.

"Your family didn't have a cook?" he asked her curiously, and she knew what he was thinking. After seeing the beach house, after seeing the Montefiore financial statements, they could have hired out.

"I was a good cook," she said more than a little defensively. "And my family has weird ideas about money and responsibility. Mom went to Woodstock. My grandfather is on the top-ten list of donators in the country."

"Actually, that kinda makes sense."

"You've met them and you think that?" asked Catherine. "Wow."

"Where's your father?"

"I never knew him. He died when I was young. It's just me, my mother and my grandfather. That's all that's left of the Montefiores."

He studied her, not saying anything, and she met his eyes, not looking away. The cool gray darkened two shades to midnight, and her nipples tightened two shades to easy. She didn't taste her food. Her stomach was too tight. After they ate, the waiter cleared the dishes, and she wondered whether Daniel would stay with her all night. Sadly, that was what she had regressed to. The conversation was slow and stilted, and all she could think of was feeling his body pounding into hers.

Her thighs quivered.

Hussy.

She was ready to get up, to take her tiny bit of pride and leave, when the man at the table next to them began to speak—loudly.

"I've had it, Nicole. You're starting once again. What is it this time? Global warming? Terrorism? Hurricane season getting active?"

"Keep your voice down," Nicole insisted.

Catherine looked at Daniel. He picked up a cocktail napkin and pen.

*Do you want to leave?*

Catherine took the pen and was going to answer in the affirmative, but then the man began complaining again. "Why should

I? Do you think I care what these people think? In fact, I think they should know what I have to deal with when I'm with you."

Catherine looked at Daniel and smiled politely. "I'm not ready to leave yet. The food is really good. We should have dessert."

He nodded.

*Just say when.*

"When I'm around you, I'm depressed all the time. I want somebody happier. Cheerful. I'm a half-full kind of guy, and you're the one who says that not only is the glass empty, but the water's been contaminated by chemical spills, and you're going to die, so why even try?"

"That's not true!" the woman yelled back.

Catherine picked up her water glass and sniffed carefully. Daniel saw her, and his mouth cracked into a smile. Shyly she smiled back and took a long drink.

"That's what I perceive the truth to be, Nicole. It doesn't matter whether it's real or not. It's what I think is real that matters. You don't listen to me."

*I can see why,* Catherine wrote, penning a quick cartoon of a baboon with tiny ears.

*Typical man,* he wrote. *I apologize for the whole of mankind.*

Nicole's face was flushed, her eyes blinking back tears. "That's because you only see what you want to see. It doesn't matter if there are toxins in the water or not, even though most of the time I'm right. Do you remember when you wanted to eat those canned artichoke hearts and I told you not to? I saved your life."

"I wouldn't have eaten the hearts. I'm not stupid."

"I think we should order dessert," said Catherine, smiling gracefully at Daniel.

"I heard the tiramisu is exquisite."

"You're tempting me," she said, and she meant to talk about dessert, she really did, but she wasn't talking about dessert anymore.

Apparently he figured that out because his jaw tightened, his nostrils flared, and she could feel the responding wetness between her legs. Like Pavlov's dog. Next to them was World War III, but right now, she felt as if she were floating, light-headed and breathless. Completely aroused, she was contemplating even bigger and bolder steps when Nicole began arguing again.

"Ha. You're not listening to a word I'm saying. I'm just the white noise in your life, aren't I? It doesn't matter how many times I have rescued your sorry ass, does it? Next time, you inspect your own food."

The man's eyes narrowed dangerously. "Now you're getting mean, Nicole. Find some patsy who's happy with your mother-complex."

"Sondra Barnes doesn't mother you, too?" Nicole shot back, and Catherine cheered, even if she didn't know Sondra. It was time that Nicole stood up for herself.

Jack's face whitened. "What's Sondra got to do with it?"

"Oh, come on. Do you think I'm blind? Always staring down her shirt, always tucking in your stomach. Do you think she'd go for a retread like you?"

"She already has," he spat, pure venom in his voice.

Catherine flinched.

"Don't do this, Jack," Nicole begged, tears now spilling unchecked from her eyes.

*She should leave him,* Catherine wrote.

*She loves him,* Daniel wrote back.

They both glanced at Jack, wondering what he was going to do, before cautiously looking away.

"You're going to make a scene, aren't you? Make me out to be the jackass." Jack looked around the restaurant, noticing the eyes carefully not staring in their direction. "She drives me to this. I swear."

"Jack. I love you." Nicole half rose, but Jack had his mind made up, and if he didn't leave, Catherine was ready to help him.

"Too late, Nicole. Pay for your own freaking dinner. I'm not hungry anymore." Then he stood, threw his napkin on the table and left. Nicole promptly began to sob in earnest.

Catherine made a face at Daniel. Should she help? Oh, yuck, she was never any good at people things. However, the waiter beat Catherine to it, coming over and giving the woman a glass of wine.

Not that wine was going to fix a broken heart.

Nicole took her napkin and wiped her eyes. Then she drank her wine and stared silently, the tears streaming down her face again.

Torn, Catherine looked at Nicole, picked up the pen, but then began to sketch. Eventually, she had a passable sketch of Jack, sprawled on the floor, an open can of artichoke hearts oozing onto the wooden floor.

Daniel watched her as she drew; she could feel his eyes on her. "Can I see it?" he asked after she put the pen down.

"Is it awful?" she asked.

"I think you should give it to her," he told her, quite sincerely, too. She could tell. That's what she liked about Daniel. He didn't say anything he didn't mean.

"I can't give it to her." Catherine didn't like to share her art. It made her nervous, and open, and bare, but then, compared to Nicole's situation, those things didn't seem so bad.

Daniel looked at her, his eyes encouraging. "Yes, you can. I think she'll treasure it forever. And sign it. It'll be valuable someday."

"You think?" she asked, liking the way he thought.

Daniel nodded, and Catherine felt flush again.

"You're good for me," she told him, because he gave her courage. When she was with him, she thought she could be a trailblazer.

His eyes cooled. "I wish I was good for you." Then he nodded to the sketch. "Give it to her."

Obediently, Catherine took the napkin and passed it to the other table.

Nicole took one look, and then stared. Then she laughed. It wasn't a healthy laugh, more hysterical than anything, and Catherine looked at Daniel in alarm.

"Trust me," he whispered across the table. "That's completely normal."

After Nicole regained her composure, she managed a smile. "Thank you. I'm sorry to interrupt your dinner."

Catherine waved a hand as if it happened all the time. "No worries."

Daniel paid the check and Catherine noticed that he picked up the tab for Jack and Nicole, too. It was all done discreetly, and she wouldn't have noticed except for the brief conversation with their waiter.

Catherine frowned at the wayward pull of her heart. She already suspected that he wasn't good for her. Yes, he wanted to be good for her, but merely wanting it wasn't enough. She knew that. He knew that, too. It was there on his face.

"Ready?" he asked.

He had no idea how ready she was.

Once outside the heavy doors of the restaurant, the building was nowhere near as welcoming. Tall stone pillars were everywhere, the marble floors echoing every word, every footstep, every thudding beat of her heart. Catherine locked her arms around her waist. Time to go home.

"Thank you for dinner. I wasn't sure what to expect, but I had a wonderful time." She wasn't sure whether to kiss him, shake his hand or to simply walk away. While she was pondering the social implications of going on a date with a widower, he took her hand.

"Thank you for the company," he responded, his thumb pressing intermittently against her palm. It wasn't a conscious gesture, almost nervous, like bad Morse code, and she smiled.

"What?" he asked.

"It's nothing," she said, right before he kissed her, his mouth hungry and warm, so seductively warm. He drew her closer, until she couldn't breathe. She didn't want to breathe; she was drowning in this, drowning in the luxurious waters of a man's kiss.

Catherine parted her lips when his restless hands glided over her, across her hips, around her waist and along the curve of her back. Everywhere he touched, it was like hot liquid pouring over her skin. But there was no pain, only marvelous heat.

She could feel one of the pillars at her back, cold and hard. In a split second, he had shifted them behind the pillar, out of the light, into the shadows, where it didn't matter if he was good for her or not. This was good.

Her hands slipped around the brawny sinews of his back, sliding up and down, betraying her thoughts. She loved this, touching him and kissing him, and in a moment, kissing wasn't nearly enough. His mouth went from hers to her neck, the rasp of his stubble skimming her throat, and she shivered, relishing the delight. His hips pressed against hers, and she could feel him there, between her legs, until she was dying to moan. Boldly, his hands slid underneath her dress, cupping her rear, pressing her closer, which was throwing gasoline onto an already-blazing fire. She felt so hot. So drenching hot.

The hands slid lower, sliding between her legs, and he touched the damp silk. She felt her whole body tense rigid as a bow. Instead of rushing her, his thumb slid back and forth, slow, steady and merciless, until her eyes closed, her head weak and languorous. Oh, this felt so good. Too good. This time she did moan, quietly, carefully, but she knew he heard.

•

He whispered against her neck, things she understood only too well, the insistent pressure killing her. Music spilled out over the building speakers, old Barry Manilow, and it seemed wrong to feel like this, and she wanted to laugh, but as the piano keys crashed in her ears, she didn't want to laugh, she wanted this. Only this. His hands slid the fabric aside, and he was touching her there, and her hips moved, grinding against him, harder and harder, her muscles tensing around his hand. He moved faster, and she could feel his body grinding, as well, and it was pretty much sex in clothes, but she didn't care. Right now, she just needed to come. Badly.

His other hand lifted the back of her dress, the cold stone against her bare skin. Her muscles locked, frozen, as he stroked her faster and faster, and she was close. So very, very close. She could hear the sound of a zip, not hers, and she exhaled.

Oh, yes, yes, yes.

But right when she was ready to explode, right when he was about to enter her, there were voices there in the lobby, echoing voices, and a violent shock ripped through her. No. She needed to come. She struggled to breathe, the voices getting louder, the crescendo of the song's refrain building, and she felt Daniel adjust her dress, his hand pressing her harder and harder, and his mouth settled on hers.

"Come," he whispered against her lips. "Come," he ordered, his voice covering hers, his tongue not so seductive, purely carnal, and helplessly she obeyed, shattering apart.

The voices continued to complain about the hot weather, about making plans for a dinner next week at Nobu, and asking after an uncle who'd been ill. Catherine tried to breathe deeply to force oxygen into her lungs.

While the idle chatter droned on, and the crooning sounds of Barry Manilow changed to an up-tempo Avril Lavigne tune, Daniel put their clothes in order. He pressed his forehead against her own. Finally, thankfully, the voices went away, and they were alone again. Daniel took a step away from her. The distance firmly back in place.

"I can't do this," she whispered, holding a hand to her chest, her heart ready to explode.

"I didn't mean for that to happen," he said. "I shouldn't have done that."

She stared at him, his gray eyes bitter. "What do you want?" she dared to ask. With only a little bit of encouragement, she would risk this. Sometimes she did things she shouldn't do, either.

"I want you."

Such simple words. Such difficult words. If she didn't ask any more questions, she could interpret those words however she wanted to, but Catherine wasn't stupid. "You want an affair? No emotional commitment, no sharing, no ties?"

Daniel wound a hand through his hair and took a quick breath. The shadows of the building couldn't disguise what he was battling inside. He looked at her then, the conflict seemingly resolved. "That's all I can do."

Not the answer she had hoped for. "That's not me."

"I know," he said, and when his expression softened, she put up her hand.

"Go. Just leave before I change my mind."

THE PHONE WAS RINGING when Daniel walked into his apartment. He picked it up, wanting to hear Catherine's voice.

"I know it's late, but I thought you might be up."

Claudia. Frustrated, Daniel collapsed onto the couch, his body still aching. "I always have time for you."

"Thank goodness Michelle married you," his mother-in-law answered.

Daniel quickly changed the subject. "Are you all right? Do

you need something? Some repairs on the house?" Claudia live in a fifty-year-old house on Long Island, the house that Michelle had been born in, and a house that Daniel had repaired because that was his family, too. He and Michelle had worked together for three years, dated for almost a year, and been married for five months, but Claudia would be his family for life.

"No."

"Is this about the anniversary?" he asked, aware she knew which one he was talking about.

"I hate it. Every year I don't go, and every year I feel guilty for not going."

"I know," he said, because he spent every September eleventh in a bar somewhere. Always somewhere new. He couldn't tell her the pain and the guilt would go away because he wasn't sure they ever would.

"I was talking to Stella Mancini this morning, and she made me so mad, telling me that it was past time that I moved away from New York. I don't want to move."

"Don't move, then," he told her, rubbing tired eyes.

"Maybe she's right. She said I should find a condo in Florida. Something around Tampa, and get away from the city. Stella said there were too many bad memories for me here and as long I stay in the shadow of Michelle's death then I'll never get back to normal. Those were her words. 'Get back to normal.' Like I can ever get back to normal. What is normal? Tell me, Daniel. You buried a wife. I buried a daughter. Are we ever going to get back to normal?"

"No," he replied. There was heaven, hell, and then there was purgatory. That halfway place where nothing ever changed, time didn't move and everything was comfortably numb. Right now, purgatory was as close to normal as he got.

"Is Stella right, do you think? Do I need to move?"

"What did you tell her?" He didn't want Claudia to move. She was his link to Michelle, and he needed her just like she needed him. Claudia didn't have anyone else but him. Michelle had been her only kid.

"I told Stella that I'd talk to a Realtor. So I did. Do you know how much I can get for this old place now?"

"You're going to sell the house?" he asked, and his pulse jumped nervously.

"You don't think I should, do you?"

"That's not my decision to make, Claudia." His fingers pulled at the fabric of his pants, his face carefully controlled, even though there was no one to see him.

"Are you ever going to move from that apartment, Daniel?"

"No." It was his home. Their home.

"I don't know what to do."

"Do what you need to do."

"I don't think Michelle would have wanted me to leave Long Island. This was her home, too. I was looking through my pictures yesterday and I couldn't find her graduation pictures."

The graduation pictures. Daniel remembered those. Cap, gown, on-top-of-the-world grin? Check. "I think I have those. We put a lot of things in storage, but I haven't touched them."

"Could you get them for me?"

Storage. He didn't want to go to storage. It was dusty, and cold, and untouched.

"Okay," he agreed, and she must have heard the uncertainty in his voice.

"You don't have to do this, if you don't want to."

"No, no. It's fine. There're probably a lot of pictures, Claudia. Do you want me to get all of them for you?"

"Yeah. In case I move. I'd like to have what you'll let me have."

"I'll look for you," he promised, feeling the sweat on the back of his neck. "Is next Saturday okay?"

"That'd be perfect. You don't think I should move, do you?" she asked him again. Claudia needed him.

"It's your decision. I can't make it for you." He would always be there for her though. That's who he was.

"I wish…I wish so many things. I keep thinking that I should have grandchildren. I have a cross-stitched birth announcement without a name. It needs a name…." Her voice grew quiet, and Daniel closed his eyes. People expected him to be the strong one.

"I should stop talking and let you go to bed. You're a good son, Daniel. The very best."

Daniel hung up and stared at the wall where all of Michelle's pictures hung. Their wedding day, Michelle standing in front of Niagara Falls on their honeymoon, Michelle pulling a beer at the bar. Five months. They'd only been married for five months. Daniel assumed they had all the time in the world. His mouth twisted into a deep frown.

Daniel walked into the bedroom, carefully putting the wedding ring back on his finger where it belonged. And when he woke up, he reached for a woman who wasn't there.

# 9

THE WEDDING RING was back in place.

The next morning, Catherine saw Daniel on the elevator. She stared at the scarlet and gold threads of the rug, picking out the curling arabesques in the curvilinear pattern. Her eyes did stray once. To his hands.

Catherine's stomach cramped. However, she survived day one.

Wednesday, day two, dawned and she saw him again. This time, on the fourth floor. Catherine had gone there to ask Montefiore's high renaissance specialist about a Cellini sculpture scheduled to be auctioned on the weekend. The appraisal rooms were wide-open spaces with desks here and there, unopened crates and objets d'art scattered in a seemingly haphazard manner, which actually did make sense, once you knew the system.

Yuri was deep in conversation with one of the cataloger trainees, so she waited patiently. When an auction featured a particular period, those specialists were always swamped.

While she idly picked through an old catalog on Yuri's desk, Daniel walked in, and began talking with Eamon, one of the senior jewelry appraisers. Catherine skulked two small steps in his direction, curious. Every time she saw him, he was so put together. The tie neatly knotted. The shoes black and polished. Shirt starched. No hot burn in his eyes—they were coolly impassive, and she missed the heat.

She leafed through the pages of the catalog, not really looking. Not close enough to overhear, either.

Daniel came up behind her and the tender skin on the back of her neck pricked. "You can ask, if you want to know," he said quietly.

"No. It's not my business," she told him, keeping her eyes firmly on the Bronzino painting in the catalog, *Neptune,* the strong contours of the sea god's shape, aloofness of the subject, the cool color tones.

Daniel dropped a ring on the picture. "My brother found this at his bar. I told him I'd try to track down the owner."

*It was an engagement ring. The man seemed to be drowning in rings.*

"Oh," she answered casually, picking it up, the metal still warm from his touch. "It looks like Oliver Cummings. Platinum. What did Eamon say?" She dared to look at him, noticed the gray eyes warmed to silver.

His mouth curved up. Not quite a smile. "Oliver Cummings."

"You should go see them. They're on Park and Fifty-seventh. The store's been there forever."

"Do you want to go?" he asked.

Catherine shook her head. "No. I've got work to do."

She dropped the ring back on the catalog, hearing it fall with a satisfying thump, and wheeled around to leave.

"Catherine," he said, and she stopped, turned.

"What?"

"I could use your help. I'm trying to do the right thing and find the owner."

Why couldn't this be easier? Why couldn't she forget the feel of his skin against hers, kissing his mouth? Why did her pulse race every time he was around? But it did. *Get over it, Catherine.*

"We'll go late this afternoon," she said, her voice firm. *Good job.* "Just before closing. You want to do the right thing? I'll help. That's all."

"I know," he said softly.

She felt his eyes on her as she walked away, but he didn't say a word.

DANIEL WAITED FOR HER outside the Montefiore building, staring up at the dark gray sky. The summer heat showers had already come and gone, leaving behind a trace of rain that evaporated nearly as soon as it touched the ground. He pulled off his jacket, pulled off his ring and waited.

She breezed through the doors, hair flying, shirt wrinkled, wearing a skirt that covered up way too much of her legs. As usual the hard-on came, but Daniel was prepared, and ruthlessly tamped it down. Control. That was all. Then he smiled, not really caring if the humidity was dank, if September was coming in seven days, if the entire world went bottoms-up. Catherine was here.

"I have to get back soon," she told him, killing any of his expectations right up front. Her eyes were nervous, her mouth starting with a firm frown, then softening to not quite a smile. Beggars sure couldn't be choosers, and Daniel would take what he could get.

Conversation was limited in the cab ride over. Her hands had a stranglehold on the hem of her skirt, clasping and unclasping, against the long length of her legs. A more unscrupulous man might notice the way her chest moved as she breathed, remembering the creamy swells that stopped his heart. She noticed him noticing and folded her hands under her arms.

"How's the audit going?" she asked, picking a subject that could hack a man's libido to bits.

"Fine," Daniel answered, lying. All the financial reconciliation in the world wasn't going to change the numbers. While he started digging through the financials, the computer specialists at his firm had investigated everyone who had access to control the commission structure.

The sales team who set the commissions, the vice presidents who could alter the commission structure, Catherine and Andrea Montefiore, who would profit from the commissions, but all those names had been cleared. Only one remained. Charles Montefiore. And the e-mails between Charles Montefiore and Walter Chadwick—the CEO of Chadwick's—that mapped out an entire commission structure didn't help. It didn't help at all.

"Are you telling me the truth?" she asked.

He stared at the tiny map of New York in the backseat. "I don't think we should talk about this," he said, because he didn't want to see the hurt in her eyes, and he didn't want to be the one to put it there.

She didn't argue, but turned and looked out the window as the cabbie honked for a limo to move out of their way.

When they got to the jewelry store, Daniel climbed out and automatically made a move to help her, but changed his mind when he saw the way she was looking at him, as if he were the Grim Reaper, Freddy Krueger and Bigfoot, all rolled into one.

Okay. Moving on.

Cummings's store was old-style discretion, none of the well-branded opulence of Tiffany's. Michelle had loved Tiffany's and used to drag Daniel there every time they went uptown. Daniel shook his head once, and looked around the display cases, searching for something similar, but most of the jewelry was modern and free-form. The ring in his pocket—the engagement ring—was square-cut, with the rigid design standards of decades past.

Catherine held out her hand, and he put the ring there, his fingers grazing her palm. "It's definitely Cummings," she told him. "Maybe he'll be able to find the owner."

"Thank you for helping. I know it's not easy."

"Don't be silly," she said, but she didn't smile at him.

The salesman approached them. He wore a polished suit, and had graying hair and a neatly trimmed mustache that had been held over from the sixties. He looked at Catherine, looked at Daniel, and then arched a brow. "Shopping for jewelry?" he asked, in a clipped English accent.

Catherine was first to correct the man. "We actually wanted to talk to Mr. Cummings. About a ring. An old ring." She handed the piece over to the man. "We're trying to track down the owner."

The salesman pulled out a loop from behind the glass counter, and stared for long minutes. "It looks like Oliver's work. I'm sure that is his mark. However, it's probably fifty years old. At least."

"Can you look it up?"

The man shook his head sadly. "A lot of our records were burned in the seventies."

"Maybe Mr. Cummings will remember it?" asked Daniel hopefully. If this was a dead end, he wasn't sure where to turn, but he wasn't going to give up. A ring was important. Irreplaceable.

"Oliver's in Europe at the moment, but he'll be back late next week. Why don't you come back then?"

"Certainly," Daniel said, and he noticed Catherine looking curiously at the rings in the display cases. He wanted to tease her, but it didn't seem right, so he watched her—not that it was a problem. To Daniel, her face was fascinating. She didn't smile easily, watching the world carefully, but he understood that. Most of the time, the world deserved to be watched carefully.

After a few minutes, she straightened and nodded politely to the salesman. "We'll be back," she said, and that was the end of it. Daniel watched her walk, watched the curve of her ass, and his body jerked. It lasted only a second before he could restore control.

Catherine never noticed.

Outside, Daniel was ready to signal for a cab for her, when he saw a little girl in pink shorts and top standing frozen on the sidewalk. Big blue eyes silently crying. He tried scanning the crowd for a mother, father, nanny or some responsible parental unit.

None.

Catherine didn't hesitate. She ran directly over to the child, crouching to her level, diving right in.

"Did you lose somebody?" she asked, and the little girl didn't answer.

"We should call a cop," suggested Daniel, standing far away. Sometimes he scared kids. They liked people like Gabe or Sean, with friendly faces and easy laughter. Daniel wasn't even close.

Park Avenue wasn't the best place in New York to lose a kid. Park Avenue at 6:00 p.m. was an even worse place to lose a kid in New York. Everywhere, stores were closing, and people were heading home. Daniel pulled out his cell and dialed 911, and told the operator about the situation. She got his name and location, and promised a cop would be there shortly.

Two seconds later, the cops arrived, but the little girl still wasn't talking. He watched as Catherine tried to coax information out of her, watched as the cops tried to coax information out of her, but she wouldn't speak.

Catherine looked up at him, her face worried. "It'll be okay," he promised, knowing he had absolutely no control over anything, and it was probably a stupid thing to say.

"You should try and talk to her," she suggested. Daniel shook his head. "If she won't talk to you, she's not going to talk to me."

One of the cops looked at him as if he was a hard-ass, but Daniel wasn't about to freak the kid out any more than she already was. However, now all eyes were focused on him, condemning him for being a mean-hearted bastard. All eyes including the little girl's.

Oh, fine. They wanted to see him fail?

Daniel bent down and gave her a half-smile. Probably looked like a fool, but she didn't seem scared. Her hair was brown and long, tangled with bits of what looked like yellow candy.

"Did your mom take you to the candy store?" he asked.

Slowly she shook her head.

"That's not candy in your hair?" he asked, trying again.

This time she nodded.

"Did you come from the candy store?"

She nodded again.

"Who did you go to the candy store with?"

Her mouth tightened, and she considered him with eyes that killed his heart. "Daddy."

"See, she likes you," said Catherine.

"I probably look like her dad," he muttered. "Do I look like your dad?" he asked the child. She shook her head. *Hell.*

"There's a kid's store a block over. We can take her there," the cop answered. "If it's her dad, he probably didn't even notice she took off."

Catherine rested her hand on his shoulder, reassuring him.

Daniel looked at the little girl. "Do you want to go back to your dad?" he asked, and she nodded her head. Daniel stood, and handed over responsibility to the cops. *Finally.* "Okay, I think this mystery is solved."

"You should go with her," said Catherine, ignoring the fact that the cops had the situation under control. That was their job.

"I'm sure they wouldn't want a stranger interfering," said Daniel, waiting for the cops to agree with him.

"If you don't mind," answered the first cop, shooting down Daniel's theory. Come on, couldn't they figure out that he wasn't any help? Sweat trickled down the back of his neck.

Catherine looked at him, clearly expecting him to go along with this. And how was he supposed to refuse that?

Daniel forced a smile on his face. "Fine. Let's go."

And the five of them walked down Park, over to 57th, down one more block before arriving at the colorful storefront of Dylan's Candy Bar. Figures.

There was a tall man standing out front, his hands over his eyes. "Kaitlyn!" he yelled as soon as he saw her. The little girl ran to him, and Daniel stayed back. Catherine glanced at Daniel curiously.

"Want to get a drink?" she asked, and he knew that wasn't a good sign. It was the interrogation. He could feel it. Daniel pulled at his collar, but nodded.

The tiny pub was around the corner, but the ambience wasn't important. He ordered a beer, bought her a glass of wine and settled in the chair across from her.

"Thank you for helping," he said. "I'll see Cummings when he's back from vacation."

"What was that?" she asked.

"What?" he answered.

"With the girl."

"I'm not used to kids," he replied, taking a long, cool swallow of beer, dodging her eyes.

"Okay," she said, and that would be the end of it. That was Catherine. One strike, and you were out. She wouldn't try again, and he felt like a heel.

"Michelle wanted kids. She wanted a little girl because she liked girl clothes, all that pink stuff. She had a name picked out, Anastasia, for the princess, because that was what Michelle was like. Everything was a fairy tale. Anyway, I told her we should wait for a while. I got screwed in that deal, too. It seemed like I made wrong decisions all over the place."

Catherine stared at him. He didn't want to drag her into this. He didn't like this merging of his old life with her. He wanted to keep them separate, but that was becoming impossible. "I'm sorry," she told him, as if she were responsible. "I shouldn't have made you help."

"Don't apologize. You haven't done aything wrong. You don't deserve all this."

"You would make a good father," she told him, watching him carefully with her artist's gaze.

"I had thought so at one time. I always thought my dreams were pretty ordinary—a wife, a family. Those were the sort of dreams that were supposed to come true. Did you ever dream of that?" He wanted to know about her dreams, because he suspected hers were buried so far down that ordinary people couldn't touch them.

"I wanted to be an artist," she told him, her eyes so deep that he wanted to stay there as long as she'd let him. "I'm not good enough to live up to Grandfather's standards."

"You are good enough. Your grandfather just doesn't know everything about art."

She smiled at him. "And you do?"

He nodded. "Yeah."

Daniel met here eyes for a moment longer, seeing her dreams reflected there, and then she checked her watch.

"I need to get back," she told him.

"Of course," he said, because for a second, he'd forgotten everything else. That was the best thing and worst thing about Catherine. She made him forget.

CATHERINE SPENT the rest of the week cataloging high renaissance art, and trying not to think about Wednesday. Talking about dreams was a dangerous thing. Dreams were a fluid, fickle thing. One day, she wanted to be an artist. The next day, she wanted to be in love.

Art was static. No matter how many hours you studied a painting, it didn't change, and it didn't disappoint you. It was precisely, exactly the same. Art was safe, which was why by Friday, she had developed a taste for climbing the stairs rather than taking the elevator (better on the thighs), ate lunch in her office (economic and frugal), came in late (lots of sleep was excellent for the complexion) and in general had managed to avoid seeing Daniel for an unbelievable one and one half days. She wanted to be an artist. She didn't want to fall hopelessly in love with a man who could probably never return that love.

That afternoon, she was so pleased with her problem avoidance that she changed into shorts and T-shirt and dared to walk along Riverside with her mother at lunch. The park ran north-south along the Hudson for over four miles, and when the weather was warm, like now, there were walkers, bicyclists, joggers, lovers and photographers. Of course, her mother had a severe caffeine habit, and because of said habit walked at seventy-five miles an hour, but today Catherine kept up.

Maybe she was huffing a little as they passed 145th Street, and yes, her back was soaked with sweat. Andrea Montefiore was wearing black spandex shorts and a sports bra that revealed absolutely no spare flesh whatsoever. Catherine sighed.

"Come on, Catherine," her mother called, wanting her to hurry along.

Catherine broke into a jog, abandoning all pretence of capability. Her mother laughed, and then sat gracefully on a bench. Catherine, even further abandoning all pretence of capability, collapsed. A barge chugged down the river, the steam pipe billowing, and Catherine knew just how that overloaded boat felt.

"That flush on your cheeks looks fabulous, darling. Vibrant, healthy, like good sex."

"Mother!" she exclaimed, partially because she was embarrassed, and mostly because, like the renaissance era, her sex life had, for one moment in history, been masterful, expressive, bringing humanity closer to paradise. However, like the renaissance era, it was over, done with, and was now fodder for the history books.

Her mother's teeth flashed in a grin. "Oh, don't be such a puddleglum. We're both adults."

"Well, yes, we are, but you're still my mother, and there're certain topics that you'll never hear from my lips."

"Sex being one?" her mother asked, brown eyes teasing her.

"That and the artistic influence of the rococo style. We're never going to see eye-to-eye." Catherine loved it, and passionately defended the overblown excess. Andrea Montefiore thought it sucked eggs.

"You're a good daughter."

"You're the best mother I've ever had. How's the audit going?" Catherine asked, hoping that at least her mother would tell her the truth, since no one else—Daniel—seemed to want to.

"Not well." Her mother frowned.

"You have to do something, find something," Catherine urged her. Andrea Montefiore was a force to be reckoned with. If there was a solution, her mother could find it—at least when it pertained to English furniture of the Regency period.

"I'm sure it will all work out," her mother said confidently.

Catherine looked out on the river, watching the barge move slowly, water billowing in its wake. She brushed the hair off her face and sighed. The problem with the art world was that you never had to deal with the outside world: the trash barges, the union strikes and one stubborn financial auditor who was thorough, precise and would leave no single financial document unturned.

Her mother, not sensing the impending doom, took in her daughter's Green Day T-shirt and shook her head. "We're going shopping. I'm in New York, and Londoners think they have it all, but no, it's not home. You need something a little more…passable."

"You're insulting my workout clothes?"

"Actually, I'm insulting your entire wardrobe. Come on, dear. It'll be a lark."

A lark. Ha. More like being dipped into burning lava, possibly wrapped in mud-soaked, exfoliating seaweed leaves at the same time. "I don't know, Mom."

"Consider it an early birthday present."

"Clothes? For my birthday? Oh, no, Mother. You're not getting off that easy." There was only one day out of the year when Catherine took center stage. Her birthday. After the twenty-four hours were over, she went back to her normally grounded self, but on her birthday…all bets were off.

"Your birthday? Is that coming up?" her mother asked, with almost a straight face.

"September third. Lest you forget."

"As if I could. Thirty-six hours in labor is nothing to ever be forgotten. All right. Not your birthday present, but, do this for me. Tomorrow morning. And we'll take Sybil. She has such marvelous taste in fashion."

Catherine rolled her eyes.

"I'll buy you a new bag," her mother said, sweetening the pot. "Hermès. Prada. Name your designer."

"Bribery?" asked Catherine.

"Canal Street bribery," answered her mother, going for double or nothing. Catherine had always loved Chinatown, mainly because her mother used to take her there when she was a kid—to get away, to have fun, to see the world.

Catherine's two-year-old Prada knockoff was ready to be

replaced. The zipper stuck, the seams had split and though she hated to replace it, because it was like an old friend, knockoffs weren't their finely crafted relatives. "Against my better judgment, I'll agree."

Her mother grinned. "Terrific. Now let's pick up the pace!"

Catherine wiped the sweat from her eyes. Joy.

THAT AFTERNOON, after a quick stop at her apartment for a rejuvenating shower and change of clothes, Catherine went to the top floor at Montefiore's to see her grandfather about the audit.

She had procrastinated, deferred, quibbled and debated until she had no choice.

"I'm here to see my grandfather," she told Myra, his secretary. The woman was tough, and had been guarding her grandfather's desk since Catherine had been born.

"He's on the phone. Why don't you wait, dear?" Myra suggested, peering over her glasses at Catherine.

Meanwhile Catherine double-checked everything in the Italian neoclassical giltwood mirror, circa 1780, that hung across from Myra's desk. Okay, she'd been trying to dress a little nicer. Even Sybil had said she was looking better. And yes, she might be wearing a little more makeup than normal, but that was solely designed to cover the extra circles under her eyes. This whole price-fixing accusation was killing her nerves. Obviously it was the price-fixing accusation. What else could it be?

After Myra waved her through, Catherine heard the quiet bubbling of the samovar. Ah, her grandfather was brewing tea. Catherine managed a smile.

"How're you doing?" he asked, handing her a cup.

"Fine," she said, pulling at her skirt, realizing what she was doing and stopping.

"Are you going to the auction and reception tonight?" he asked.

The reception preceded the Italian Renaissance art auction. This year Montefiore had a floor full of items to sell, eleventh- through fourteenth-century, mostly oils, some sculpture in bronze and marble and a few tapestries that they'd bought off a dealer in Florence. High dollar, great PR, lots of who's who that needed to be coddled and schmoozed. "I wasn't sure," she started, but saw the look in his eyes. "Yes. I'll be there."

"Good," he said, looking pleased with her. "I need you there."

"Mom will be there. You don't need me."

"You'd be surprised," he told her, dropping four sugars in his cup, the spoon gently stirring against the sides.

He didn't say a word, but was watching her, waiting to see what she was going to do. Charles Montefiore was like that, observant, curious.

"How's the audit going?" she asked, taking the bull by the horns and hoping it wasn't going to gore her to death.

"Not as I'd hoped," he said, and got up, shutting the door.

Catherine stared at the closed door.

"What's wrong?"

"The system's saying that our commission structure has moved lockstep with Chadwick's."

It'd only been one week. How much could Daniel know in one week? This was preliminary. "There's a mistake."

"I've looked over the statements myself. Damned computers, should have learned how to use them years ago when your mother tried to teach me."

"There's someone else doing this," Catherine stated loyally.

"I think the statements are wrong," he said.

And Catherine frowned. Her grandfather didn't "think" anything. He knew. He decided. He moved forward. There was no room for uncertainty. A client could smell uncertainty a mile away, that's what he had always told her.

"I want to help," said Catherine, no uncertainty in her voice at all.

"You're a sweetheart to offer, but I don't think—"

"Stop. I'm going to help."

"You're sure?" he asked, his voice cautious.

"Yes."

"You're not good with numbers."

"I know the commission structure. I may not be as good as Foster with the accounting system, but I know what it should look like. And then there're the old invoices…"

"The ones in storage?"

"Well, yeah," she answered. "I mean, you have to verify the numbers against something, right?"

"You're really sure about this?" he repeated, with that same piercing look he'd given her when he told her the Gainsborough was a fake.

Catherine's feet shuffled under the chair. "I'll dig out the boxes tomorrow and have them sent to Foster. He can double-check them. You know, in case I make a mistake." She closed her eyes for a second. No room for uncertainty. "Do you want me to do this?"

"What do you think?" he asked, his voice carrying across the room.

"I'm asking you, Grandfather. Do you think I can do this?"

"Maybe."

She stared at him. "That's not good enough," she said sharply.

"I do think you can."

She nodded once. "And now that I think about it, I don't even have to go to storage. There are digital images of all the invoices. I can use those. I don't know what's going on yet, but we'll figure it out."

"You think you can?"

This time she looked him straight in the eye. "Yeah. I can."

# 10

DANIEL HADN'T PLANNED on attending the Italian Renaissance art reception that night, but Charles Montefiore had insisted. He wanted Daniel to understand the full scope of the business, the financial, the social and the artistic, all coming together under one mighty umbrella that was over eighty years old. The old man was proud of the business that his family had created. If it wasn't for the incriminating e-mails between the two auction-house heads, Daniel would have thought that pride was well-deserved.

As Daniel walked into the Montefiore's reception hall, it was as if he were stepping into a museum. Everywhere he looked there was a painting, or a sculpture, or something that boggled the eyes. A peasant woman with a child, cloaked in a bright scarlet tunic. A soldier on horseback, resplendent in silver armor. A lush green landscape with a river that looked so real he could hear the steady burble as it swirled around the rocks. A dark bronze statue of two embracing lovers that towered almost to the roof.

Waiters wandered the marble floor with black tuxedos and slicked-back hair. The grand dames of society held their chins nose-bleed high as they strolled the hall in evening dresses and expensive gems to match. Daniel looked at his own suit, and decided it would have to do.

After a few seconds his eyes adjusted to the visual feast. His senses overloaded, still he knew the exact moment when she entered the hall. He had steeled himself for it, but even so, the punch to his gut had a lot more kick than he expected. All the control he'd been so proud of was gone. The blood was heading straight down to his groin.

She looked gorgeous. Her dress was classic black with a deep neckline exposing glowing, familiar skin that he dreamed of touching. Her hair was pulled back neatly in a barrette, looking about as fragilely controlled as Daniel felt. Catherine's innate sensuality threw everything inside him off balance. She seemed to hide it from everyone, but Daniel knew. He'd seen, caressed, tasted. When Catherine had lain underneath him, brown eyes wild, that soft, red mouth open and slack...

Daniel cleared his head, shaking it off.

Not the time. Not the place.

While he was weaving elaborate fantasies, she didn't even look in his direction, not once, and he knew that was on purpose. She'd made her decision. She was being smart and careful. Daniel understood smart and careful. In fact, he even approved of smart and careful. Yet he took his left hand and tucked it behind his back.

He didn't wander around, but stood quietly in the corner. He meant to watch the proceedings, but he ended up watching her, until Charles Montefiore came toward him. Not good to leer at the client's granddaughter.

"You're enjoying yourself?"

"There's a lot of art. I don't know much about it, but it's pretty."

"I'll have Catherine sit with you at the auction. She can explain how things work."

"Catherine?" he asked, because he wasn't supposed to know who she was.

"My granddaughter. Over there," he said, and then waved her over. "Recently she's taken an active interest in the price-fixing business."

She had?

"Catherine, I want to formally introduce you to Daniel O'Sullivan. He's doing the audit for us."

She held out her hand. Daniel took it for a moment, and then reluctantly released it. "It's a pleasure," he said.

"Catherine is going to help you with the audit. It seems she has some concerns."

Daniel's eyes flew to hers, wondering where this had come from, but she was watching him coolly, and he wondered if her grandfather had put her up to this. He didn't think she'd work with him willingly. *Would she?*

The old man wrapped an arm around her. "Can you sit with him at the auction tonight? Daniel's new to all this."

Daniel shook his head. "Oh, not necessary at all, sir," he told her grandfather. "I'm sure I can follow it without taking some-one's time."

"I'm sure you can, but I've got my own interests to protect here. I trust Catherine to explain it well. Will you do this?" he asked her.

Catherine's mouth tightened, but she nodded. "Of course."

Charles Montefiore gave his granddaughter a squeeze and then excused himself. "Take good care of him," he told her, and then walked away, leaving Catherine standing awkwardly with Daniel.

"Why did you decide to work on the audit?"

Catherine shrugged. "My grandfather needs me now. I don't think he knows how much he needs me, but he does. He doesn't have a lot of faith in me, and he should. He needs someone to fight and defend him. I thought Mother would do it, but she's too focused on the art to see the big picture. I can do this."

"Yeah, you can."

She turned on him then, calm and composed. "You aren't nervous, are you?"

This was new from her—this cool sophistication that shouldn't be so…arousing. He didn't think she realized it, but here, she was in her element. Here, she was all Montefiore.

"We'll deal with the situation," he said neatly, his control firmly back in place.

"Come on. If we sit in the balcony, you can ask me whatever you need to know."

He followed her out of the hall, then up the red carpeted staircase, noticing the paintings and the catalogs on the wall, trying desperately not to watch her silk-covered ass, the curves made for a man's hands. It wasn't easy not to look, and eventually he gave up trying. "It's really impressive," he said, because he needed to say something, but his voice sounded like sandpaper, and he cleared his throat.

"Thank you." She turned her head, caught him looking and promptly blushed.

"Sorry," he apologized, because he felt as if he'd been rude.

"Up here," she said, leading him into a small balcony area with a wooden railing, elaborately carved, polished to a sheen.

"This looks like a theater," he said as she led him down the row, settling in a plush velvet seat.

"An auction is theater. The atmosphere is all part of the show."

There were a few employees in the top rows, standing around and chatting. He'd noticed the employees were all in evening clothes. The women in cocktail dresses or long gowns, the men in darks suits or tuxes. Everyone looking very, very sharp. "The employees stay up here?"

"Not always. Sometimes we're on the floor. It depends."

"Are the auctions always this formal?"

"The big ones are. The smaller ones are for mostly local dealers and collectors." She leaned forward, her dress gaping an inch to expose honey-colored skin and the shadowy vee of her breasts. Instantly his cock jumped. Dear God. This wasn't like the tidy blouse and skirt she usually wore. This was not good. Heavenly, seductively, ball-bustingly not good.

Daniel adjusted his jacket, concentrating on the intricate carvings in the railing, until he noticed the wooden nymphettes were nude. Okay, not a good time.

Catherine stared straight ahead, not looking at him, not looking at his oh-too-obvious hard-on, not looking at anything.

"I'm sorry," he said again, apologizing for disrupting her peace, apologizing for getting the world's stiffest cock every time he spent a millisecond in her presence, and in general, apologizing for whatever she thought he'd done.

*Time to change the station, Daniel.* He took a long, cleansing breath, tearing his eyes away from cavorting nymphs with full, lush, bountiful… *Stop!*

"When you have an auction, it's from several suppliers?" he asked her, casually, easily, not thinking about her lush, bountiful breasts at all.

"Usually. Sometimes it's an estate. Those are the ones that get courted. Grandfather has been courting the Drexels for years. Chadwick, Montefiore and Smithwick-Whyte's all have."

"And the commission structure comes into play to secure it?" Oh, that sounded intelligent. Professional, even. Daniel managed a half smile, still ignoring her breasts.

"It's a negotiating point. As well as the estimated proceeds, where the auction is placed on the calendar, the publicity given an auction. It's all part of the game."

Two women came down the row, seating themselves next to Catherine, and he saw her flinch. One didn't wait for introductions. "Hello. Sybil Aston. Damn glad to meet you."

The other girl held up a hand, not nearly as forward. "Brittany."

He waved back. "Daniel."

Sybil whispered something in Catherine's ear and Catherine's hand tightened on her thigh. He didn't need to look at her thighs. He really didn't. But they were covered in black slinky fabric, completely opaque, he couldn't see a thing. His memory knew. His cock jumped again. Discreetly, Daniel folded his hands over his lap.

Thankfully, Charles Montefiore appeared at the podium. He introduced the auctioneer for the evening, a well-fed gentleman with a crisp British accent, and the first item was brought out. A sculpture of a man and woman passionately embracing. Daniel bit back his groan. This was not fair on so many levels.

Catherine looked at him strangely, and he needed to regain his focus. "The accounting system shows all the transactions matching Chadwick's," he said, leaning into her, only partially because he didn't want to disturb anyone else.

"The system is wrong," she said coldly.

Okay, that was better. Unless he tilted his head a couple of degrees, he wasn't staring down her dress anymore. "You think someone put in the wrong data?' he asked, noticing her perfume. It wasn't the same scent she had used at the beach. This was stronger, heavier, muskier.

And…he was back to sex again.

"Look at the invoices and see for yourself," she said, crossing her legs, her hands tightly folded in front of her. Body language indicated there was no sex on her mind. No, all the desperate tension currently unrolling in Daniel's body was a solo effort.

"Foster says the only invoices left are the digital copies," he said, leaning closer still but it was the perfume's fault, not his.

"He's wrong. The originals are in storage," she said, and he saw her roll her shoulders, her chest rising, nipples perked against her dress. Catherine rubbed her arms.

*Maybe not so solo.*

"Cold?" he asked politely. "You can have my jacket."

"I'm fine."

"Can you show me the originals?" he whispered, stealing a furtive whiff of her neck.

Her eyes closed, and her hands glided over her thighs, stroking. Daniel ground his teeth together, until he heard them scrape. "I'll talk to Foster. The boxes are in the archives across the river. He can get them."

"You don't need to talk to Foster. You're supposed to be helping me. You show me," he said, his lips feathering against her ear. She had marvelous ears. Soft and downy, with tiny diamond studs. She didn't need the dress. Just those tiny diamond studs. And maybe heels.

"I won't," she answered, her voice cutting through his momentary fantasy.

"Why don't you do it anyway?" he asked, and he curled his hand around the armrest because he wanted to touch her so desperately, and this wasn't the time to touch her.

"Is this business or personal for you?" she asked, staring at his hand.

He looked at her squarely. "Both. I trust you. Most people lie to an auditor. You learn to pick who you work with." It was the truth. He trusted her more than he'd trusted anyone in a long time, and he knew she'd never lie to him. And then there was the fact that he seemingly liked Charles Montefiore, and then there was the last bit. The one that had his body completely fossilized.

She met his eyes and didn't blink. "*We'll* get them."

"Thank you."

"I haven't changed my mind about you," she murmured in his ear, and Daniel closed his eyes. He was supposed to work like this? Oh, yeah, that was his job. Still, if he could have her again, the excruciating pain would have been more than worth it. Seven years of celibacy took a hard, hard, nail-chewingly hard toll on a man. He hadn't realized it until now.

Daniel exhaled, clearing her scent from his mind. "Okay. That's your decision. We can start on Monday."

"Can you work tomorrow afternoon?" she asked.

He could work tomorrow afternoon. He could work tonight. In fact, he could work right now. "Anxious?"

"I want him cleared," she said, and he could read the doubt in her eyes, the worry in her face. Such a soft touch. Hopefully, her grandfather would be cleared, but Daniel wasn't so sure.

He reached out and touched her hand. "I know."

"So, WHAT WERE YOU whispering about?" teased Sybil after the auction was over, and Daniel was safely gone.

Catherine shrugged. "He had questions about the business."

"It was all business?" Sybil asked, her eyes disappointed.

"Completely," said Catherine, even though the muscles in her thighs were starting to shake from holding them so tight. Tension, what a killer.

"We're going to McCarty's," said Sybil. "Want to go?"

McCarty's was the bar down the street from Montefiore's, a mix of college students and the young professionals who worked in the area. On another night, when Catherine didn't feel so...tight, she would have gone. However, right now she wanted to go home alone.

"Not tonight. I've got some work to do," she answered, fumbling for an excuse.

"Now?" said Brittany, black brows shooting above her black frames.

"Just reading. There's a new Dürer, and I picked up some reference books from the Met. That'll put me right to sleep," she said, smiling happily.

Sybil shook her head. "I don't know what's up with you

lately, Catherine. You're turning dull. If I didn't know your secret hankering for drawing naked guys, I'd be worried. You *are* still drawing naked guys, aren't you? Please tell me you haven't given up your only vice."

Catherine laughed. "Don't worry. Not giving that one up."

After they left, Catherine walked down the one block to her apartment. She needed the night air, she needed the time to shake off the aftereffects of the amazing Mr. O'Sullivan. He was sneaky, and devious, and completely underhanded.

He'd never been flirty before and tonight he was definitely flirty. The moments were subtle and small, but they were there. Touching her, whispering in her ear, devouring her with those hungry eyes—as if she couldn't read exactly what he was thinking. *Exactly.*

It wasn't right. She'd made her decision that she wasn't going to have a steamy, hungry, passionate affair with him and she thought he respected that decision. Before tonight, Daniel had been aloof and brooding. When he was like that, she could maintain her distance. But this subtle flirtiness? She was toast.

Very sneaky.

And to remind her how sneaky and devious and completely underhanded he was, she went home and spent the evening sketching him without clothes. It didn't help. She finally went to bed, her hands snaking under the covers. Pretending it was him. That did help some, but not enough.

AFTER THE AUCTION, Daniel went home and took a long, hot shower. Cold showers were his usual thing, but tonight he needed to feel the warmth, the scalding heat. He stood under the spray, eyes closed, her perfume still floating in his head. The water burned down his chest, and he could feel her touching him, stroking him. He braced a hand against the tile, grateful for the steam that hid so many weaknesses. Her lush mouth brushed against his neck, his stomach, and he moaned, low and loud, because here, he was hidden from everyone.

Her hands were like velvet against his skin, and he could feel the blood stirring and boiling inside him. Feelings. So many feelings, so many sensations, pelting down on him, beating against him, harder than the water, hotter than the water. His hips moved back and forth, slowing pushing, slick flesh surrounding him, and it was almost as if she was there. So good, so full, so strong. He moved faster, one hand tracing over the tiles. Slick water gliding down her rich breasts, full hips.

He wanted…

Daniel opened his eyes, hot water pouring over his face. No matter how he tried, he was still alone, touching himself in some bastardized imitation of human contact.

When he came, Daniel's roar was long and anguished.

# *11*

THE NEXT MORNING, he woke up, reached out to touch her and immediately remembered his promise. Daniel pulled his hands back firmly under his pillow.

After he dressed he headed out to the storage building in Queens where the photographs of Michelle were. It had been nearly nine years since he and Michelle had been here last. His wife had loved Christmas, had boxes upon boxes of Christmas things, none of which were designed to fit inside a one-bedroom apartment.

He had kept the key to the padlock on his key ring, as if there could be a storage emergency and he'd need to get there in a hurry. The worst part about being painstaking and careful is in the case of an actual emergency because it's impulsive and thoughtless that saves the day. Painstaking and careful doesn't get you shit.

Daniel jerked open the door, the rusted metal groaning like a long-forgotten ghost.

Amid all the extra furniture, the boxes were exactly where they had put them. He spotted a Christmas-tree box, three red-and-green boxes of ornaments, a cardboard box of wrapping paper, probably long ruined, and Michelle's Elvira Halloween costume from before they were married, sitting in the corner. He couldn't picture Catherine as Elvira. Diana, goddess of the moon, yes. Sleeping Beauty, yes, but Elvira? No. Slowly he got the necessary boxes out, shoved them into Cain's truck that he'd borrowed and drove back to Manhattan.

He spent the next two hours sorting through the pictures, making two neat piles. One for Claudia to have, one for him to keep. The Claudia pile was getting bigger and bigger until he realized what he was doing. So he carefully pulled out some pictures from her pile, the ones of Michelle at New Year's, the ones of Michelle trying to pour drinks at the bar and the last ones that he'd taken the day she bought a digital camera. Vibrant and alive, she stared at him as if he were the only man she would ever love.

Eventually Daniel had adjusted the numbers, so that his pile and Claudia's pile were exactly even.

In fact, by the time he was finished everything was back in balance.

CATHERINE SPENT the morning at Barney's with her mother and Sybil. The pink and black fashionista destination of choice was the perfect backdrop for Sybil's pink sundress with strappy heels. Her mother was in her suit—Armani, her favorite. As a matter of protest against such refined taste, Catherine wore a white blouse and jeans, if only to remind them that she was the stylistically challenged stray in the bunch.

Andrea Montefiore, when given an ounce of encouragement, could shop like a woman possessed. Sybil provided way more than an ounce. They piled Catherine's arms high with sweaters and shirts, and slacks, and skirts, and shoes, and Catherine struggled along behind them, not saying a word.

Finally, Andrea turned, giving her daughter her best appraiser's stare. "I think that's it."

"Thank you. My arms have stretched a mile."

Sybil laughed. "You are such a wimp."

"Yes. Yes, I am. I wear the wimp banner proudly."

Sybil pointed to the dressing rooms. "Go forth, so we can see what we've done."

By the time Catherine had put on the fourth skirt, her mother frowned. "Why doesn't that hang right on you?"

Sybil tapped a finger against her cheek. "Are you lopsided?"

"No, that's your vision," teased Catherine. "Handbag, mother."

"I'm getting hungry," said Sybil, who had never had a buttercream-cupcake fetish in her life, and was probably thinking of salad.

"Canal Street," Catherine said, firmly standing her ground. "We'll get a knockoff and Chinese, all at the same time." Quickly she checked her watch. She was supposed to meet Daniel at two, but assuming they were efficient, she could make it with plenty of time to spare.

Sybil shuddered in horror. "Knockoff? No one said anything about Canal Street. Do you know how many designers are starving while you buy the cheap merchandise for the masses?"

"It'll be fun," answered Catherine.

Her mother shrugged, looked at Sybil. "I did promise."

Catherine nodded. "This is the start of the run-up to my pre-birthday birthday. Learn to deal. When it's your pre-birthday, we'll hit Saks or Soho, your choice. Promise."

Sybil sighed, knowing she was beaten. "Canal Street, here we come."

THE SHOPS IN Chinatown were set up with storefront after storefront featuring row upon row of purses, bags of bright silk clothes in shiny red and royal blue, round paper lanterns in pink, square paper lanterns dripping with gold tassels, ivory figurines shaped like elephants and ancient warriors and elaborate daggers studded with jewels. The colors of a drunken Picasso, and the thrown-about style of post-Imperialistic China. Somehow it all worked.

Catherine looked at her mother and smiled, but Sybil kept scanning the crowd, praying she wasn't going to run into somebody they knew.

The owner of the first store was a little old lady, who led them to a tiny room in the back where the good stuff was—a smorgasbord of fake Prada, fake Hermès, fake Gucci and some fakes that she didn't even recognize.

"I stand by my earlier position and am dissenting on principle," stated Sybil.

"We won't be long," said Catherine's mother, taking a cigarette from her purse and sticking it between her lips.

"No smoking," muttered the owner, because yes, you can break all the New York City laws with knockoffs, but no smoking laws are strictly, *strictly* enforced.

"It's all right," said Catherine, defending her mother. "She doesn't really smoke. Nerves," she whispered, as if that explained it all. Her hands stroked the buttery imitation leather, fondled the gold-plated trim and caressed the lopsided double CC logo. When you grew up in an auction house, forgery was one of the seven mortal sins.

In Catherine's world, handling a fake was like watching an R-rated movie when she was thirteen, scarfing an extra three cookies from the cabinet or being so gullible as to believe that if it looked like a Gainsborough, it might actually be a Gainsborough.

She was deciding between the faux Gucci and the faux Chanel when the shouting broke out. The old woman scurried to the front of the shop, slamming the metal door behind her.

Catherine, her mother and Sybil were locked in.

"What the—" said Sybil.

*Uh-oh.* "I think it's because of the police," said Catherine, acting calm, because she knew the drill here. Sybil was a rookie when it came to dealing with crime and corruption. The gates were shut until the cops disappeared, and then voila, the gates were rolled back up, and the mad buying and selling started all over again.

Sybil's eyes appeared to grow four times their normal size. "We're going to get arrested."

"Oh, please," Catherine said confidently, acting as if she were the expert. "We're safe as long as the gate stays down. Give it ten minutes."

It was a good twenty minutes later and there was no sign of the old woman. The charm of being locked in a sardine can of a store in the last days of August was starting to wear off. Especially without the A/C.

Catherine's mother fanned herself, her perfectly applied Elizabeth Arden makeup starting to melt. "I think I'm going to faint."

While her mother melted, Catherine idly weighed the benefits of the faux Prada against the faux Chanel, thinking that maybe she was going to get the Chanel after all, if only because the lopsided logo vaguely resembled her butt. "It'll only be a few more minutes."

"Maybe it's not the police. I think we should call them," stated Sybil. "Or someone."

"Not the police. Bad idea," said Catherine. "I bet that'd make the papers. Members of Montefiore's caught with fake merchandise. Again."

Sybil rolled her eyes. "You're the only one who's ogling the fake merchandise."

"Am not." But Catherine regretfully put the purses aside. Sybil was probably right. "We could call Grandfather. He'd come and let us out." She looked at her mother.

"You want to explain this to your grandfather?" shot back her mother.

"No," said Catherine. She looked at Sybil. "What about your family?"

Sybil arched a brow beyond her hairline, eyes narrowed in street-fighter fashion. "No one will know I was here. Ever. I will make each of you swear in blood."

Okay, no help there. They were stuck.

Another thirty minutes went by, and Catherine was starting to get worried. She was supposed to meet Daniel in an hour, and if the woman didn't appear soon, she was going to be late. She should call him at Montefiore's, but Sybil was only two inches away, with that piercing X-ray vision that could probably spot a fake Gainsborough at twenty paces. Catherine decided to wait.

Even Sybil was sweating now. Her hair was slightly mussed, her complexion wan. "Do you think the owner'll come back soon? I can feel my blood pressure rising." Sybil said, smoothing her hair back, mussing it up even more.

Catherine checked her watch. Two o'clock, straight up. They'd been here for an hour and a half. "Any second now," she said, and knew she was going to have to call Daniel. At least tell him something. If she was businesslike and professional, Sybil wouldn't catch on. After all, this *was* about work.

Right then, her mother muttered something colorful and foul, and Catherine looked at her in surprise. "Does that mean I can say that, too?"

"No," her mother snapped, her mouth crippling what was left of the cigarette's remains, but at least she wasn't smoking. They really needed to get out of here soon, or her mother was going to take out the matches.

Catherine pulled out her phone. "I was supposed to meet the auditor this afternoon. Now, in fact. Let me call and tell him that I'm running late."

She opened her mobile and dialed the after-hours switchboard at Montefiore. "Daniel O'Sullivan, please," she said, trying not to blush, because wan, mussed Sybil was watching her with X-ray eyes.

"He's a total babe," Sybil whispered to Catherine's mother, just as Daniel answered.

"O'Sullivan."

"Uh, this is Catherine Montefiore."

"Yeah, I figured that one out."

"I've been detained."

"Chickened out, didn't you?"

"No," answered Catherine, keeping a tight smile pasted on her face. "I'm just stuck."

"In traffic?"

"Mmm-hmm."

"I can wait."

"There's no need for that."

"It's okay, there's no traffic in New York that's that bad."

"It might be some time," she said, her voice slightly stressed.

"Where are you?" he asked, hearing the stress.

"Chinatown. There's been a bit of a problem."

"Do you need help?" he asked, because he was that type of man.

Sybil, obviously listening to the conversation—the snoop—nodded her head desperately.

Catherine shook her head at Sybil. "No, there's no need. Really," she said, with heavy emphasis.

"Catherine, what's going on? Are you hurt? I can come down there."

"Everyone's fine."

"Everyone except your mother, who's going to pass out at any moment," added Sybil.

"Who was that?"

"Sybil Aston. You remember Sybil from last evening at the auction."

"Ahhh…" he said, a wealth of meaning in one tiny utterance.

"We can reschedule at a time that's more convenient," she told him, completely professional and businesslike.

"Of course—assuming that you want to reschedule," he said silkily, and she bit her lip. Now he wanted to flirt? Why now?

"The audit's very important to me and to the company," she answered back.

He was silent for a moment. "I know," he said, and then gave her his cell number. "Are you sure I can't help?"

"Positive."

After that, she heaved a sigh of relief. Mission accomplished, and Sybil didn't catch on to a thing.

"You like him?" asked Catherine's mother. At first Catherine assumed she was talking to Sybil, but then she realized the question was addressed to her. Not having appropriate armor, she stuck the faux Chanel bag against her chest like a shield— a fake shield, crafted in the finest imitation leather, but a shield nonetheless. She looked at her mother, chomping at the cigarette, no longer Armani cool.

"He's nice," said Catherine. "Very professional. Well-mannered." *And he has a body that not even Michelangelo could have crafted.*

Sybil pushed the damp hair back from her face. "I'd hit that."

Catherine's mouth fell open. Shocked. *Shocked.* "You'd sleep with him, not caring one way or another about how he felt about you?"

Sybil looked at her in amazement. "Sure."

Catherine looked at her mother. "What do you think about this?"

Andrea Montefiore pulled the cigarette from her lips. "I'd hit that, too."

*Oh. My. God.* "Mother!"

"I'm sorry, Catherine. But it's hot as hell in here, and I think we can be honest."

"But he's—" *heartbroken, faithful to the memory of his wife, and obsessively tenacious* "—nice."

"Are we talking about sex here?" asked Sybil, stuffing the stack of soft-side messenger bags behind her head and crossing her ankles. "If so, what does nice have to do with anything? Is it so wrong to have a blood-pumping, bedpost-shaking, hoo-haw busting sexual experience and not be emotionally involved?"

"I think so," said Catherine weakly. "People get hurt that way."

"Catherine, Catherine," said her mother, shaking her head sorrowfully, and—*oh God*—Catherine knew her mother was two seconds away from talking about sex again.

She threw a faux Prada clutch in her mother's direction. "I don't want to hear this. Not. A. Word."

"Grow up, Catherine," her mother muttered.

*Grow up.* Spoken by what she now considered two malfunctioning adults trapped in the sardine can. So now the question became, were they right?

Catherine hugged the Chanel knockoff close to her chest, and contemplated a future that contained blood-pumping, bedpost-shaking, teeth-rattling, hoo-haw busting sexual experiences—hers for the taking.

But that wasn't Catherine. Catherine was "sensitive" and as such was too fragile to deal with that sort of emotional quicksand.

Oh, that was such crap.

She was scared.

Scared that Daniel would give her the once-over and then toss her out like a worn Prada hobo with a broken strap.

But that wasn't Daniel. Maybe there were men in the world like that—tons in New York—but not him.

Emotionally crippled? Yes. Hard-hearted? Nope. Not a chance.

The man was as much a soft touch as…her.

Catherine started to smile.

"Well, glad to see something perked you up," her mother said.

Catherine was saved from a response by the two thumps at the metal gate, and then slowly, blessedly, it creaked upward, and the old woman appeared.

"Yes!" exclaimed Sybil, standing up, dusting off her dress.

The old woman looked at Catherine. "You take the Chanel?"

Catherine looked at the bag, noticed the white dye that was coming off on her hands. She glanced at the woman and grinned. "Mom, you owe me a bag. Pay up."

DANIEL SHUFFLED the pile of printouts in front of him, but it didn't matter how he realigned the piles. Everything was the same. Three months of imaged invoices exactly matched what the accounting system said they would, and unless somebody could pull a rabbit out of hat, or a Rembrandt out of a garage sale, Montefiore and Chadwick were about to get busted for collusion. Once was maybe a coincidence, but six months' worth? No way.

It was going to kill Catherine, and he knew it.

With a heavy sigh, Daniel put his desk back in order, stuffed some papers in his briefcase and pushed the chair back neatly where it belonged. An hour from now, he was supposed to work at Prime. This day just couldn't get any worse.

ON SATURDAY NIGHTS, the bar was a meat market. There were no other polite words for it, only some words that Daniel didn't like to think about because they reminded him of how ancient he felt. Sean loved it, though—he adored women. Everything about them. Cain was tending at the side bar, with Sean at the main bar in the back. Daniel shouldered through a group of androgynous goth types, past a cluster of women in tanks tops and shorts, past the pack of business suits, until he finally broke free. The first thing Daniel saw was that the tarp was still up and covering a good quarter of the rear wall. Not a good sign. Sean was pulling beers, pouring shots and making a hundred women deliriously happy, all at the same time.

"I thought you were going to solve the permit problem so that Gabe could fix the wall," Daniel yelled above the crowd.

Sean pulled his hands off the tap and lifted them helplessly. "We're still officially a historic building."

"I'll be downstairs," said Daniel, hoping to elude bartending duty tonight. He wasn't in the mood to deal with lusty females on the make and the surly males who chased after them. There were times that Daniel didn't mind the games, but right now, he was no better than any other surly male in the bar, and his balls had been twisted into an ugly shade of blue. All in all, he wasn't a happy guy.

He took the steps downstairs two at a time, until he rounded the corner where he caught Gabe and Tessa locked together, his brother's hand halfway down her ass, and Daniel rubbed his eyes.

*Not now.*

He coughed, loudly, and they sprang apart. "Sorry," murmured Tessa, color high on her cheeks. Gabe just shrugged.

*Jerk.*

Ah, crap, thought Daniel, because he didn't want to be mad at Gabe for being happy.

"I'll go," offered Tessa. "I was only here to get…uh, limes." She headed for the stairs when Gabe stopped her.

"Limes?"

"Right. Sorry," she said, pulling out a box of limes and then dashing upstairs, Gabe watching her with love-struck eyes.

"I was going to work," Daniel said, as a way of apology for interrupting. He wanted his brother to be happy. He knew Gabe and Tessa were meant to be together. In fact, he'd done his part to get them together. Sometimes, though, it felt like ten thousand bamboo shoots right under the nails. "I saw Cain upstairs. Is that all right?" he asked nicely, politely, brotherly. *Excellent work.*

Gabe nodded. "Are you okay?"

Daniel looked at his brother. "Why do you ask?"

"I don't know. Just curious."

"I'm fine."

"How's work?"

Daniel stared, trying to figure out why Gabe cared about his work. "Why?"

"You've been so busy."

"Oh, yeah. It's this audit," he answered, uncomfortable with the way Gabe was staring at him. "Sean says we're still a historic building."

"Yup. He thinks the holdup with the permits is coming from the mayor's office, but why does the mayor's office care about a bar? A city of eight million people, and they have to mess with my bar?"

"Sorry."

"Nah. I'm only whining. Let me go upstairs, before Sean decides to leave."

"He's getting off early tonight?" asked Daniel. He didn't want to close. He didn't want to stay in a dark hole, staring at a computer until 4:00 a.m.

"Don't panic. I need you to cover the back bar after Cain leaves, but that's only eleven to one. You can handle two hours, right?" he asked, making Daniel feel like a jerk, once again.

"Absolutely. Let me get the payroll done, and I'll be with you."

He was halfway through the checks when his cell rang, the ID blocked.

"O'Sullivan," he answered.

"Daniel?"

It was Catherine.

"What are you doing?" she asked.

"Nothing," he said.

"I changed my mind. I want to see you."

"When?" he asked, instantly alert.

"Now?" she asked, her voice so soft he barely heard the words. "Is that a problem?"

"No. Not a problem…oh…" he muttered, remembering where he was, remembering what he was supposed to be doing.

"It's a problem. Never mind," she said, and he hated disappointing her.

"No! Wait. It's not a problem. I swear."

"If you have plans or something—"

"No plans at all. I'm sitting here, doing nothing. Hanging out. Watching some TV. Nothing. Honest."

Gabe would understand, or Gabe would understand if Daniel told him the truth, which he had no intention of doing because they wouldn't understand about Catherine. They would think… well, he had no idea what they would think, but whatever they thought, it'd be wrong, and he wasn't ready to deal with that because he didn't know what to think himself.

Catherine needed him. That was all that was important right now.

"You can come over?"

"Yeah. Just tell me where to go."

After he hung up, he stared at the computer screen for a second, the numbers blurring there. He twisted the gold band off his finger, and tucked it in his pocket. It was getting easier and easier to take off, and Daniel didn't want to think about what that said about him, about the feelings that he'd once had—still had—for his wife.

Catherine needed him. He should change first. Shower. Maybe cologne. No, not cologne. That was too much. Then he was taking the stairs two at a time, and spotting Gabe working next to Sean. Tessa was sitting at the bar, joking with both of them.

"I have to go," he told Gabe.

Both brothers stared. "Now?" asked Gabe.

Daniel looked around at the crowded bar. "Yes," he said hopefully.

"Why?" asked Sean, eyes suspicious. That was Sean, always thinking the worst. This time, he was right. "Why?" Sean repeated.

This time Daniel was going to have to give an answer. "Work."

Gabe looked at him skeptically. "It's Saturday night. What accounting crises occur on Saturday night?"

"Bad, bad, really bad ones."

Gabe sighed. "Go. We'll cover. Tessa can bartend."

"You will owe me significant favors for this one, Gabe," she snapped.

Gabe laughed, and they shared a look. "And you'll love every minute of it."

For a second Daniel stood, unable to move, watching the two of them, so together, so not alone. Daniel was tired of being alone, as well.

# 12

IT TOOK ONE HOUR, twenty-seven minutes and thirty-three seconds for the buzzer to ring, and in that one hour, twenty-seven minutes and thirty-three seconds, Catherine did nothing but stare at the door, her heart pounding like an out-of-body experience, as if the throbbing organ was sitting across the room and she could hear it beat, watch it pulse.

She buzzed him up and closed her eyes, praying this was the right thing. A moment later, Daniel was at her door, holding a briefcase and wearing a dark suit. Okay, maybe she hadn't been clear. She hadn't specified what she changed her mind about. Maybe he assumed this was business. His gaze raked over her for a second, taking in her dress, the cute white toeless pumps on her feet.

"Come on in," she said.

"Did you want to go out?" he asked, his voice carefully polite, his feet firmly planted behind her threshold, his locked jaw looking as if it were seconds from breaking.

Catherine hesitated because it was time to either put up or shut up, and decisions had never come easy to her. Finally she shook her head once, and she watched his chest expand as he exhaled. He came in, and she shut the door, and they were alone. Uh-oh, who went first? He was the man, but she was the hostess. Should she offer him a drink? All she had was tomato juice and some out-of-date milk. Oh, gosh, she was going to make him sick. She couldn't even wing this. Catherine looked at him helplessly.

"I—" she began, and didn't get any further. Thank you, Daniel.

He grabbed her, pinned her against the door and was kissing her as if there wasn't going to be tomato juice, or milk or even tomorrow, which seemed like a fine plan to Catherine. She wasn't ready to think about tomorrow, so she poured herself into this, into him. His fingers dragged through her hair, pried against her jaw, and her knees threatened to give out.

His hands dug under her dress, lifting her, raising her skirt, and she locked her legs around him, feeling him heavy against her. He smelled like sandalwood and whiskey…and Daniel.

Days, it'd been only days, and it felt like years, eons, as if whole entire eras had passed. She had missed this.

"Catherine," he gasped against her neck, and she couldn't breathe, she could only feel him between her legs. She ground herself against him, he felt so good, so…full. Daniel swore. "Condoms. I brought them. Wait," he muttered.

He braced her, and her hips moved automatically, the friction drenching her panties with the feel of it. Were his arms shaking, or was that her? She was shaking. Yes, she was definitely shaking. It was cold. It was hot. Her heart was going to explode. That's it, her heart was going to explode.

She heard the rasp of his zipper, heard the deafening rip of her panties, and then…

For a second he froze. She stopped, too, her mouth stuck ingloriously open. Her eyes met his; his gray turned to full-on black.

And Daniel was inside her.

He began to move, his big chest heaving with effort, his hands urgently kneading through what was left of her underwear, and this time, she felt the urge to talk. Very, very, badly.

All these days had turned her into a raving lunatic.

"Please, yes, no, there, oh, oh, oh, oh…"

She heard her shoes fall to the floor, echoing like two shots.

He moved in closer, so there was nothing separating them. Not air, not skin, and he buried his face in her hair, at her neck, his breath heavy in her ear. He was muttering, whispering, groaning—their bodies making the sharp, wet sounds of sex.

His thrusts were harder, deeper. And she wanted even more. She told him so. Oh, man, she'd *told* him so, she'd never talked like that in her life, and he made a sound. A laugh. A gasp. But he knew, and she stopped trying, she just needed to feel, to absorb.

To come.

Oh, yes.

She could feel it, feel it ripping up inside her....

He pressed once, twice...

Catherine exploded.

Her legs slid down his thighs, wobbly, and he grabbed her when she started to fall. He swore, picked her up and carried her to bed.

"I'll be one second," he said, and she adjusted her clothes, making herself decent again, but then he was back and he sat down next to her.

"No," he said, gently brushing away her hands as she tried to make sense of things. He unzipped her dress, his hands so marvelously tender, and she was still shaking. Then he helped her out of her clothes, fingers gliding over her, touching her, caressing her, and she was glad it was dark. It was so much easier when there were no lights, when she couldn't see in the shadows, only feel. She used to live to see, but this feeling stuff...sweet.

He unclasped her bra, his mouth taking one breast, then another, and Catherine smiled to herself. Oh, this was nice. So pleasant and easy. His hands slid her panties down her thighs, and she sighed. Everywhere his hands lingered, on her hips, her knees, even her feet. It was her own bliss.

His mouth came back to her mouth, kissing her, lingering, his tie tickling her breasts. He was still wearing a tie, she thought, giggling happily. He played at her neck, her ear, along the curve of her throat.

"Do you have a dawn line, too?" he asked, his lips skimming down her torso.

"Yes," she replied, wiggling when she felt the stroke of his tongue against her stomach.

"Where does it end? Here?" His fingers slid between her thighs, pushing her legs apart. His mouth stayed on the curve of her belly, playing with her naval, and she felt so heavy, so thick…so ready.

"Here?" he asked. He moved his mouth lower, his tongue finding the fine line between her abdomen and her…

"Here?" he whispered, and put his mouth on her.

Catherine jerked up. He really shouldn't be doing this. She wasn't all smooth down there, her thighs were really too big and he wouldn't last. He couldn't last….

Oh…

He pulled her skin, suckling her in his mouth, and her head fell back against the pillow again.

His tongue stroked there, and her hips bucked.

He laughed.

Her feet slid up the bed, heels digging in, sliding back and forth, matching the strokes of his tongue, and her hands fisted in the sheets.

Daniel added a finger, and she bucked again. His other hand moved to her hip, and this time it stayed there, keeping her locked in place, while he continued…

Sending her to paradise.

Her heart wasn't in that good of shape. Chocolate, buttercream frosting, cream…her arteries were probably already…

Oh…

*Oh…*

Her mouth fell open again, and she took great gulps of air, trying to breathe. The air—it was too thin, there wasn't enough of it.

His tongue began to move faster, and Catherine cried out, her calf muscle locked tight, while her heels slid into the bed, and she needed to move, she needed to escape because she was going to explode again.

Oh…

Oh…

Her pelvis bucked up against his mouth, totally inelegant. And her breathing was so loud, so…soooooooooo…

Oh…

Her back arched high, and even his grip couldn't keep her on land. And she stayed there, floating for a long moment, until finally her body landed back on the mattress, her muscles unclenching but…

"Oh, no, no, no."

Daniel bolted up. "What's wrong?"

"Leg cramp," she said through gritted teeth. "Right. Calf." Oh, she should be working out.

His thumbs dug into her calf muscle, digging in deep, and for a second the pain was killer, but then it began to fade and she watched his concerned face. He was still wearing a shirt, tie and pants—he'd lost the jacket somewhere—and Catherine grinned, her heart pulling and stretching along with the muscles in her leg.

*She could so easily love him.*

How could she not love him? How could she stop herself from feeling like this? She wasn't sure that she could. She'd never met anyone like Daniel. Someone who believed in her, someone who supported her, someone who desired her, and someone who understood her.

If only his heart weren't already taken. At one time, Catherine wouldn't have the confidence to believe that she could steal his heart. Not anymore. He gave her that confidence, and he probably didn't even know.

If they were starting new, she knew that his heart would be his. Unfortunately, he wasn't starting new, and the very thing she loved about him—his steadfastness—was standing in their way. He wasn't a man who could forget his wife. Ever.

The pain in her leg had disappeared completely and Catherine felt tears pricking at her eyes. Tears. Now wasn't that the icing on the cake?

Daniel laid down next to her, stroking her hair, her face, kissing the tears away. "I'm sorry it hurts," he whispered, and he thought she was crying about the muscle cramp. She let him think that, but managed to smile at him.

"I'm so sorry about that. I don't usually get leg cramps. Never. Ever." She hoped he wouldn't hold it against her.

"Don't worry," he said. "I didn't mean to, uh, cause it."

"That part was fine," she told him, because it had been way more than fine.

His tie brushed against her stomach, and she snickered. "You can take off your tie if you want."

He looked up at it and the nicely wrinkled shirt. "Oh. Sorry." She looked at him and grinned, then began to laugh. And Daniel grinned, and then laughed, too. She'd never heard him laugh before. He had a nice laugh. Deep and throaty and his chest moved with the force of it.

He took off his tie and his shirt and she was once again exposed to the perfection of his chest. Her hands reached out to touch him and then she realized what she was doing and one hand dropped back to her side. He pulled her hand back. "It's okay."

"I'm sorry," she said.

"You don't need to apologize."

"Good." Her hands were at his fly. "Because now we need to talk about the pants."

He laughed, and undressed, and this time when he slid inside her, it was amazing. And as his body moved, she met his eyes. It wasn't easy to stay there, and her gaze slid away, but he took her chin in his hand, and made her. Watching his face, she knew he was taking things from her, stealing things, and he didn't have a clue what he was doing to her, making everything she'd ever wished for come true.

When she came, after he curled her against him, she could hear the steady beat of his heart and she wondered if it would ever be hers.

His body stirred, one leg trapping one of hers. Not sexual. Comfort. "Why did you change you mind?" he asked. "I didn't think you would."

"I listened to some people that I trusted, and I realized I was stupid and scared. I can't know what's going to happen, but I won't be afraid of it anymore."

"I need to tell you something."

"No, you don't," she said. She didn't want to hear anything that could spoil this moment.

"Yes. Yes. I do." And she knew he was going to be stubborn and ruin everything. He was honorable, damn him. Catherine pulled her mouth into a tight line, and slid out from under that warm and inviting thigh.

He rolled to his side and faced her. "I know you think that this is about the sex, and that's great, but when I'm with you I want things that I never thought I'd be able to want again."

That was so not fair. It wasn't honorable or noble or high-minded. It was devious and completely making her hope, and she didn't want to hope, because hope was a Gainsborough landscape that was still fake no matter how badly she wanted it to be real. Her hands twisted in the covers. She would have to do this, to listen because that was the cost of having blood-pumping, bedpost-shaking, hoo-haw busting sexual experiences with the man who held your heart.

He looked at her, searching. "Aren't you going to ask?"

Catherine shook her head, refusing to give in to this. "No. Because then I'll want things, too, and I don't want to want things. I don't think that's smart."

Their eyes met, and this time he didn't have to hold her there. He could have said so many things, but he didn't. Instead, he went in for the sex.

Blood-pumping, bedpost-shaking, hoo-haw busting sex.

"You make this so easy," he whispered, kissing her, his mouth on hers as if he needed her. She knew he did, but not how she wanted to be needed. He made love to her once more, and she had to steel her heart all over again.

Damn him.

DANIEL'S PHONE was ringing. He could hear it, but he had no idea where it was. He had no idea where he was. He was in a strange bed, with a woman. And he had no clothes. And his phone was ringing.

Oh. Right.

He looked over at Catherine, and his mouth inched up at one corner.

Then the phone rang again.

Phone. Get the phone.

*Nah. Ignore it.*

The phone stopped ringing, and Catherine stirred, her smile sleepy, and he sat there in bed watching her hands uncurl, watching her legs stretch, watching her come to life.

Daniel smiled.

Then the phone started ringing again, and he swore.

Daniel found his pants tossed over to one side, and pulled out the cell.

*"Where are you?"*

It was Sean. His brother. The lawyer brother.

Daniel stood and walked into the other room where he wouldn't disturb her. "At home, why?"

"Gabe was worried. He thought you'd still be out drunk in a bar somewhere. Yesterday was August twenty-eighth, and that's not a date you'd go out and get drunk on, so I knew that couldn't be it, so I'm standing in the middle of your apartment, and wow, imagine that, you're not here. Not in the closet. Not in the bathroom. Not in the bedroom. Not even on the four-by-ten-foot balcony. What's her name, Daniel? Gabe might be sucker enough to fall for bad accounting emergencies—it's a good line, by the way—but I'm a lawyer, I deal with liars all day. Nothing gets by me, brother."

"I don't want to talk about this now," said Daniel, and Catherine appeared in the doorway. Nude. He swallowed, collapsed into a chair, the blood draining from his head. "I really don't want to talk about this now."

"When do you want to talk about it, Daniel? You're sleeping with somebody—after seven freaking years—and you're not going to let us know?"

Cautiously, he watched her. She was walking toward him, hips swaying, sun dappling her body in gold, and oh how he really loved that body. His mouth started to water, and as a man currently unclothed, she could easily see what was going on with his anatomy. Knowing Catherine, she'd want to draw it all.

"It's nothing that should concern you, Sean," he said, turning his eyes away from the light because he needed to converse intelligently. Sean wouldn't be put off for long, but then Daniel saw her kneel down in front of him, her hair falling over his thighs, and her mouth closed over his cock.

"Ahh…ahh…ahh…ahh. I have to go."

"Tomorrow. Meet me at the club."

"Yeah," he gasped, punched the off button with unseeing eyes, and then the phone fell uselessly to the floor.

IT WAS SOME TIME later before they made it to the Montefiore offices with the documents. They'd both showered, changed and hit the archives, where they retrieved forty-three boxes of invoices. Montefiore sold a lot of stuff.

They unloaded the boxes in the appraisal area, where there was space to work, although since it was Sunday, there was hardly anyone around. Daniel kept digging through papers, staring at them, but it took a few minutes for him to remember what he was supposed to be doing.

He was distracted. Completely understandable. Catherine had changed into jeans and a button-down blouse. Every now and then, as she knelt over the boxes, looking through the invoices, she'd pull her hand through her hair, letting the strands run through her fingers like water. It was the most fascinating thing he'd ever seen.

"What happened yesterday?" he asked.

She blushed. "You don't want to know."

"Yeah, I want to know."

She told him the story from Saturday, and he found himself cracking up again. "I would have come and got the three of you out."

"I know," she said, meeting his eyes for a second, before looking down at the invoices again.

"Why didn't you ask?" he said. He wanted her to know that she could count on him. Maybe he couldn't give her everything that she wanted, but he could come and rescue her from Chinatown. In the big scheme of things it was peanuts.

"I didn't want to assume things," she said, her head firmly down.

And why couldn't she look at him, either? Was it so hard for her? Daniel sighed, and went back to digging through the documents. No matter what he did, he was going to lose, and he knew it. She knew it, too. *That* was why she wouldn't look at him.

This time when he went to concentrate it was a lot easier. "Pull May of last year. That's where the commission structure starts matching Chadwick's."

Catherine read the labels, and slapped a thick pile of papers down on the desk. "May was a good month."

"That's okay. We start, one at a time, Catherine. It's not as bad as it looks."


FOR TWO HOURS they poured over documents, and Daniel was silent as he worked. Thorough, meticulous and completely focused on the task at hand. Catherine, not so much, until she found her first positive sign.

"Here," she said, pushing the paper in front of him, her finger lasering in on the last few lines. "It's from the McCory silver lot. If my math is right, and it might be wrong, they're not the same."

He took it, studied it and then looked up at her with a frown. "The original is lower. Why artificially inflate the numbers for the books?"

He had a point. As financial schemes went, this one wasn't long on brains. "We're a privately held company, so it's not to please the stockholders. All it does is make my grandfather look like he's inflating profits."

"Your grandfather's bonus structure is based on the profit number. High profits, he makes more." There was sadness in Daniel's eyes when he said that, and she didn't understand why he would be sad when they were talking about her grandfather…unless he thought her grandfather did it.

"My grandfather wouldn't steal from the company that bears the family name," she defended, wanting to hate him for suspecting, wanting to hate all his passive indifference to everything in the world. But sometimes indifference was the best elixir to pain. That, Catherine understood.

"I'm only here to look at data. Nothing more," he answered, and she stared back at him, reflecting all that passive indifference, no matter what it cost her.

"There are other people who have a similar bonus structure," she pointed out, just as objectively. "I'm pretty sure. I think. No, I'm certain. Definitely certain."

Oh, that was good, Catherine.

"Yeah, there are other employees on the same structure, some of the VPs, some of the lead appraisers, but nobody makes your grandfather's numbers." In his expression she saw so much she didn't want to see, truths she didn't want to face. He didn't flinch from any of it.

"I don't want bad things to happen to him," she said quietly, staring down at the paper in front of her.

"I know," Daniel assured her, which seemed to be as cheerfully optimistic as he got. Then he pulled out the next invoice. "And here's another one. Anderson furniture. Thirty-five thousand for a chair? Jeez, these people are nutso."

"The invoice?" she asked patiently.

"Sorry. Same thing, though. The original commission listed is lower than what both the system and imaged invoice show," he said, and then slid the paper on top of the "wrong" pile.

Catherine stared at the boxes and sighed. Two out of twenty. "We're going to have to go through all of these, aren't we?"

Daniel nodded once. "But don't worry. Time flies when you're having fun."

THEY'D WORKED THROUGH most of the night and were only on June. Ten hours and they'd done exactly two months. Her eyes were starting to blur as if she'd been staring at a Vasarely for too long, and all the colors had run together. Catherine was exhausted. "I can't do this."

Daniel was sitting on the parquet floor surrounded by neatly stacked piles. His shirt was half-unbuttoned, the sleeves rolled up, his jaw covered with a dark, sexy stubble. "Why don't you go home?" he suggested, the late hour deepening his voice. He looked up, met her eyes and Catherine shivered, a trickle of warmth dripping down her spine, a trickle of warmth dripping down her thigh. She shifted uncomfortably.

"You're going to stay?" she asked, not wanting to sound like a wimp, but sounding like a wimp. Besides, he looked tastier than any cupcake she'd ever had the pleasure of devouring.

"I want to get through another month," he said, taking out an invoice, his eyes processing it, then putting it aside.

"When are you going to sleep?" she asked.

"I'll manage."

No. She shook her head. He needed rest, he needed sleep, and she needed…something that didn't involve sleeping. Her thighs trembled, and Catherine began to smile.

Could she do this? She studied him from under her lashes, and he was completely engrossed in the numbers. Uh-huh. She could do this.

She undid a few buttons on her shirt, and went to sit next to him.

"I'll stay, too," she said, and watched his eyes flicker down her chest.

"Okay." And his gaze moved back to the paper. Okay, harder than she thought, but not impossible.

"Is it warm in here, or is it me?" she asked, flicking another button open.

Daniel slowly put the stack of invoices down in front of him.

"It's definitely getting warmer," he said. "What are you doing?"

Catherine pulled a sad face. "It's my grand attempt at seduction."

His mouth twitched. She liked the way his grin crept slowly onto his face. "Catherine, you don't have to get fancy. All you have to do is breathe, and I'm pretty much there."

"Really?" she asked, pleased, and his hands went to work on her shirt, pulling at the last few buttons. Then he rolled her underneath him, and she gave herself up on a sigh.

"Oh, yeah," he said, and then went about proving it.

# 13

EARLY MONDAY NIGHT, and Daniel wasn't looking forward to a game of racquetball with Sean, but there was a penance for everything. For lying to his brothers, and, according to Sean, for keeping secrets. An hour-long inquisition from his brother the lawyer seemed harsh, although Daniel had been through worse.

He would survive, and surprisingly enough he spent the hour kicking his brother's butt all over the court, which was cause for suspicion. Sean was normally better than this, but he was missing balls, falling down like a clown, and in general, throwing the game like a two-bit amateur.

After the hour was up, the two brothers relaxed in the club's lounge, Sean donning his courtroom face. Daniel was now going to have to pay.

"Who is she?" asked Sean. "Did you meet her at Prime?"

"Why is it any of your business if I'm seeing somebody?"

"So, you are seeing somebody."

Daniel stopped for a second, rubbed the ring on his finger and considered his answer carefully. "Maybe."

Sean slapped him on the back. Hard. "Way to go, Daniel. And it only took seven years. Is this serious, transitional or purely recreational? It can be any of the above, and I'll still be fine with it."

"It's none of the above," answered Daniel. He couldn't categorize Catherine. She wasn't transitional, she wasn't recreational and he'd never get serious with anyone again, so that left some limbo state that seemed to work best for his conscience.

"Can I tell Gabe?"

"No."

"I think he knows, anyway. Ever since you backed out of poker he figured something was strange. And the drinking binges are disappearing. You missed Michelle's birthday last night, and we both thought that was a huge step."

*Michelle's birthday?* He'd forgotten about her birthday? August 28th. Oh, man, he'd slept with Catherine on Michelle's birthday. That sounded so wrong. Claudia had probably left a message for him on his answering machine. He should call her and take her out to dinner, or something.

Sean noticed the look on his face.

"It's only a good thing," Sean said, and then ordered a couple of glasses of sparkling water. "It means you're putting your past behind you."

"Loving someone isn't something you put behind you, Sean. It's forever." Daniel looked down at his wedding ring, felt the familiar weight and for today it was okay.

"She's not coming back, Daniel. What? You're going to be alone for the rest of your life? Another fifty years? Is that really what you want? You may be a loner, but you're still breathing."

Daniel rubbed the cotton towel over his face, wiping away the sweat, but not getting rid of the anger. His brother had no right to interfere in things he would never understand. Sean didn't understand love. Sean saw everything in shades of gray and degrees of guilt, but love was absolute. "I really didn't want to hear this today, Sean."

"So shut up, and listen anyway. You're my brother. I want you to be happy."

"You be quiet. I'll be happy."

"Bullshit."

Daniel stood. He wouldn't listen to a lecture from the irresponsible brother. "I didn't come here for this."

"Don't screw this one up, Daniel."

And wasn't that ironic? "Like you're the one to tell me about the wrongness of screwing up?"

Sean looked at him once, his face serious. "Yeah. Yeah, I am. I know you. You think everything should equate and make sense and it freaks you out when it doesn't. You may think you're right, but love isn't like pushing the correct buttons on a dishwasher."

"I love my wife," Daniel said and Sean swore.

Daniel left his brother in the lounge. He showered, took off his ring and called Catherine.

FOR CATHERINE, the next days were strangely odd, and strangely happy. At Montefiore's, they worked pulling invoices, and finding more undercommissioned items, which did nothing to clear her grandfather or the company.

It didn't look like price-fixing anymore, but there was definitely something strange with the books. Price-fixing would imply that the customer had been charged an artifically inflated commission, but the modified invoices indicated that the customers had been charged the normal amount and then the accounting system altered to look like a crime had been committed.

Somebody was setting her grandfather up.

Maybe the price-fixing seemed less likely now, but there were still accounting discrepancies, and the board was still breathing down her grandfather's neck, because maybe he hadn't committed a crime, but he had profited from the doctored commission amounts. As did everyone else who got a bonus.

It was all very strange, and Catherine wasn't an accountant. Daniel was the accountant, and he was expressing no opinions on the whole puzzle.

Daniel had a meeting with Foster and her grandfather where he asked them questions, but neither of them had answers, so they went back to sorting through the original invoices.

After hours was different. Daniel took her to dinner late on Monday night, and they spent most of the time talking casually about the auction business, the city, why the work from the New Leipzig school was overrated, and he told her stories about the bar.

Post dinner, Catherine invited him to her place where he spent the night. At four-thirty, he woke to go home and change and get ready for work—which was ten minutes from her apartment. She considered asking him to bring clothes with him, to save him a good two-hour commute that was completely unnecessary, but she didn't want to assume, and as much as their situation had changed, some things hadn't.

On Thursday, they went to Cummings's jewelry store because Oliver Cummings had returned from Europe.

The jewelry designer had a kind smile, was thin, gray, with silver spectacles that he wore over owlish blues, and he knew his own stuff. He took one look at the ring and sighed.

"Brianna Taylor Kelley of the Seventy-first Street Kelleys. I was half in love with her myself. She was like that. You saw her, and fell in love. Do you like this? It's very good, isn't it? I don't know why everyone is so keen on contemporary jewelry when the old styles were so much more elegant, dignified." His eyes lifted to Catherine's. "Don't you agree?"

"Yes. Definitely. Simplicity is incredibly underrated. Everyone wants bigger, and better…." She glanced over at Daniel. "You'd better stop me before I get carried away."

"Hey, I get excited about numbers. Getting carried away is okay by me," he said, and they shared a smile. Then Daniel turned to Cummings. "Do you have any idea how to get in touch with Mrs. Kelly? I'd like to return her ring."

"I'm not sure she's still alive. Let me check and see what I have on file."

Cummings scurried away and returned a few minutes later, waving a white sheet of paper. "I have no idea if she's still there, but this is the address and phone number that we have for her."

Daniel took it, and nodded. "Thanks. Hopefully that'll be enough."

Then Daniel took her to lunch, and that night he took her to dinner. And as much as she did like to eat, they really did need to discuss what was happening between them because she didn't want to get hippy-er.

When they got back to her apartment, she decided it was time to talk.

"You don't have to keep feeding me, Daniel. Actually, I'm slightly insulted."

He looked at her, shocked, and she realized this wasn't going to be easy.

"Oh, oh, that's not where I was going. I mean, I only wanted to take you out, and it was convenient—" As soon as the words were out, he winced. "Bad word choice. I'm digging a hole here. Let's start over. What do you want?" he asked.

What did she want?

That was easy. She wanted the same thing almost every woman wanted. She wanted the man whom she was in love with to love her in return—simple, trivial, no big deal.

It took every bit of her courage to meet his eyes and not look away. "Do you seriously want to know what I want? Do you want me to tell you? And if I tell you, what are you going to do, Daniel?"

She could tell he was surprised at her tone, and she could almost see his accountant's brain processing all the possible outcomes of this conversation. She wasn't the same Catherine he'd met on the beach at the Hamptons. He'd given her courage and confidence, and now he was going to face the consequences of that gift.

"I'm sorry," he said, his eyes carefully sliding away.

Tomorrow was her birthday. She wanted to tell him, but how did she tell that to a man who couldn't meet her eyes?

So tomorrow night, they'd go to dinner, go back to her place, have blood-pumping, bedpost-shaking, teeth-rattling, hoo-haw busting sex, and she'd stare up at the ceiling because for once in her life, she had a man to celebrate her birthday with, and she was dying to do those birthday things that couples do.

"Forget I said anything. I had a long day."

"I'm sorry," she told him. "I shouldn't have brought it up."

He didn't look as if he believed her, but he did look relieved that they wouldn't be discussing it, so instead, they each had a glass of wine and she gave him her 101 reasons to love Baroque. Actually, she only got to nine.

After that, they had sex.

The morning of her birthday arrived, and Catherine woke up the same way she always did, with Daniel's thigh wrapped around hers, his arm heavy on her breast.

She grew to love the moment when the sun first hit the window because there was a difference in him then—an almost desperate intensity that he worked so hard to hide. The morning was the only time she felt as if they were something more than two people having sex. All the anxiety and analysis seemed like such a small price to pay for these moments, and Catherine got swept away again, believing that everything was going to be fine.

That morning, when he held her, his heart beating fast and sure, she almost told him what day it was. Almost said the words because when he felt so close, when she saw her dreams in his eyes, she believed in them. That a real sort of sharing existed between them—ties, the whole emotional package—but Daniel had never said a word, so she closed her eyes, burrowed her head against his chest and kept her mouth firmly shut. Sometimes words weren't necessary at all.

IT WASN'T QUITE the best birthday ever. Catherine was with Daniel in the appraisal room, silently working, examining documents and comparing numbers. The steady shuffle of paper broke the silence. His sandalwood cologne tickled her nose and made her body ache in places that she couldn't satisfy in public.

"Happy birthday, dear," her mother cheerfully called to her, giving her a kiss on the cheek.

*Oops.* Catherine wasn't such a five-star hypocrite that she was going to pretend to be unhappy about this accidental outing, so she took a quick glance across the room to see how this was going over.

Not well. Daniel raised his head, watching her, his eyes boiling, but Catherine wouldn't second-guess her decision now. She looked the other way. In Catherine's book of emotional involvement, small as it was, birthdays fell firmly into sharing and ties.

"We're kidnapping you and taking you to lunch. Sybil and Brittany are downstairs waiting. I have reservations at Lever House at one."

*Lever House.* Wouldn't that be nice? Catherine smiled, as if it were her favorite place.

"I'll be back after lunch," she told Daniel. It was sort of a passive-aggressive way to deal with the situation. *You made this bed, not me, so if you're unhappy that you're lying in it alone—metaphorically—it's all your fault.* That was about as tough as she got considering he really hadn't done anything wrong.

Daniel cocked his head. "I didn't know today was your

birthday. Happy birthday," he said, in that perfectly controlled voice. If it wasn't for the cold simmer in his eyes, she'd have never known he was mad.

*Too bad.*

Lunch was fabulous. The restaurant was decorated in a sort of cubism-meets-impressionism way, designed to reflect the sunlight seeping in through the windows. Catherine had a divine meal of salmon doused in lime and cilantro, and her mother supplied red velvet cupcakes for dessert, because she knew her daughter's weaknesses well. After twenty-seven birthday celebrations, her mother had never disappointed her yet.

"So what are you going to do today?" asked Sybil. "If you don't have plans, we could go out. Hit WD-40, or there's a new pub by the university."

Catherine glanced up from her empty china plate. "I don't really feel like celebrating. Maybe on the weekend."

Her mother gave her a sharp look.

"You sure?" asked Sybil.

"Positive," said Catherine. "Got to work."

Her mother's look grew sharper.

"How's the audit going?" Sybil braced her chin on her palm.

"We're this close to cracking the case," said Catherine, bluffing her way through it all, and she noticed her mother didn't say a word.

Sybil and Brittany made their excuses and left. Catherine sat with her mother, drinking her second martini, not that she usually drank martinis, but Andrea Montefiore had very specific ideas about how birthdays should be celebrated, which is where Catherine inherited her birthday-diva-ish-ness from.

"How are you doing?" her mother asked.

"Well. The audit's well. We're halfway through November."

Her mother sipped at her martini, studying Catherine over the rim of the glass. "Is it really going that well?"

Catherine picked at the last cupcake crumbs on her plate. "I don't know. Some days I think everything will be fine, and sometimes I don't know what to think."

"I'm glad you're doing it. So is Charles."

"Really?" Catherine perked up at that.

"Oh, yes."

"Why doesn't he tell me that?"

"He will when he's ready. Give him time. He takes longer than most. It took him about thirty-five years before he told me he loved me." She looked at her daughter meaningfully. "I love you."

"Thanks, Mom," Catherine said, taking the last crumb from her plate.

"What else is going on?" asked Andrea.

"Nothing," answered Catherine casually, looking her mother straight in the eye.

"Is that why my daughter has a hickey on her shoulder?"

Catherine looked down, saw where her shirt had slipped an inch to the side and quickly shoved the fabric in place.

"Curling iron," she said automatically.

Her mother laughed. "Nice try. That might work if I didn't know that a curling rod hasn't touched your hair since 1994, when you went to the homecoming dance with ringlets. Hideous," she said with a shudder. Her mother waited, as if Catherine was going to elaborate more.

Her mother waited in vain.

"You're not going to tell me, are you?"

"No."

"Is that why you don't want to go out tonight? Do you have other plans?"

"No."

"I wish you could tell me. I wish you trusted me enough to share with me the things that daughters are supposed to tell their mothers."

"I share," said Catherine, but it wasn't easy to. She'd never been a sharer, and not just with her mother, either. She liked to keep things to herself. Privacy. Discretion. Nothing wrong with that.

"But you won't share the story behind the hickey?"

Her mother watched her with that look that mothers get when they know exactly what's going on, but they want you to say something, but you're not, and they know you're not. Mexican standoff, Montefiore-style.

Her mother took the empty olive pick from her martini glass, and then slipped it between her lips. Catherine watched the tiny piece of red plastic, as if that pick were the most fascinating thing in the world.

"Do you want me to guess?" her mother finally asked, and Catherine acknowledged her mother was a much better Catherine mind-reader than Daniel.

"No."

"I could," said her mother.

In other circumstances, Catherine would have broken down at that point, knowing that the truth was out there, and her mother knew. Catherine would have gushed on in a girly way about how cool things were, and how she thought he was really great, and how she thought he thought she was really great, but she wasn't sure yet, and it was too soon to tell.

But those weren't the circumstances.

"Don't try to guess, Mother."

"Be careful. If anyone else notices, it won't be pretty. Gossip travels fast and people see more than you think."

"I don't want to talk about this," she said. Today was her birthday.

"If you need to talk…"

Not going there. Catherine knew this was nothing more than sex for Daniel, she knew this affair was never going anywhere, no matter how much she wished, and frankly, that was a humiliation she didn't want to share with her mother—or anyone, actually.

Her mother polished off the remains of Catherine's martini and settled the check. On the cab ride uptown they discussed the latest Michael Kors satchel, which could be found for $47.99 on Canal Street, how much the Magna Carta was going to snag at auction, how her mother was going to Miami for Labor Day, and they didn't talk about Daniel at all.

DANIEL CLEARLY didn't understand Catherine's dysfunctional nature. "Why didn't you tell me?"

Yes, that was the first thing he said to her when she walked into their workroom. Not "How was lunch?" not "Welcome back," but, yes, that he thought she should have told him about her birthday.

"It's not something that you blurt out," she said.

"You could have told me." He looked hurt, disappointed. With her mother, not sharing secrets was Catherine's fault, but if she wasn't sharing with Daniel, it was because she loved him and he didn't love her. If he wouldn't give her his heart, then was it so petty for her to withhold some piece of herself?

Maybe, but Catherine guarded herself more carefully than most.

"I don't want you to think I'm, you know, expecting something from you because I'm trying very hard not to." She felt this was a nice opportunity for him to say that he'd been rethinking the situation, and she waited for those very words.

He pushed a hand through his hair.

"A birthday's a huge thing to me, and I'd rather you not know about it, because if you knew, then you'd think you have to make a big deal out of it, because I expect a big deal, and I don't want you to feel like you have to."

His mouth tightened. "You could have told me, especially if it's important to you. I should know those things."

Catherine sighed. It was *her* birthday, and his feelings were hurt? Where was the justice in that?

"It's my birthday. There."

Daniel faced her. "We're in this thing—"

"Affair," she said, choosing to clarify exactly what he'd said.

"Relationship," he corrected.

*Relationship?* That was the one word guaranteed to set her off because today was her twenty-eighth birthday, and she had wavered over whether to say anything, and now she knew that she picked wrong, and he was upset about it, and her mother had seen a hickey—a *hickey,* for crying out loud—that he was responsible for, and she'd had two martinis and a cupcake, which she probably shouldn't have after the cheese plate they had ordered, but today was her birthday.

Catherine's eyes narrowed; her mouth tightened. "Are you changing the context of this relationship *now?*" she asked, putting one hand on her hip, her most aggressive "so-there" gesture, that really wasn't aggressive at all.

He waited.

She waited.

This was his big moment. The opportunity to tell her that things had changed, and that yes, he wanted something more. But when he looked at her stubbornly, she knew that nothing had changed.

They were having sex. A lot of sex. Lots of really, really, really great sex, but there was no emotional commitment of any kind because he was still involved with someone else.

Catherine resumed working, one damned invoice at a time.

Oh, yeah, this was the best birthday ever.

THAT NIGHT, Daniel took her out on a date. It would have been nicer if he had asked her politely, with a smile on his face, but instead he told her, his face tense, his voice clipped.

Guilt was a powerful motivator.

Over dinner, he gave her a box. Small, gift-wrapped, and she felt even smaller, not quite the birthday princess moment she had been wishing for.

"I don't want you to do this," she said, handing the un-wrapped box back to him, because she didn't want to know what was inside the box, because if she knew what was inside, then she'd want to keep it, like she wanted to keep him, too.

"If I had known—if you had told me—this is what I would have done. Please," he added, and they both stared at Pandora's box on the table.

Eventually, Catherine couldn't deny him—she never could deny him anything, which was a large part of the problem—so she opened the box. It was a necklace from Oliver Cummings's shop, a diamond teardrop falling from a delicate gold chain. It was the most breathtaking piece of jewelry she'd ever seen, and coming from someone who had appraised the engagement ring given from Ferdinand I to the Princess Maria Luisa of Rome, that was saying a lot.

"It actually wasn't that hard to pick out something for you," he said, almost proudly. "Oliver didn't help me. I want you to know that. I did that on my own."

"I love his stuff," she said, not taking her eyes off the stone. The drop was such an anomaly, the artistic representation of both water—meaning life—and tears, the symbol of both pain and humanity. It wasn't cold, like the emerald cut or the brilli-ant cut, and had depths that reflected beyond the surface. It was brilliantly perfect.

"Do you like it?" he asked, and she lifted her eyes to his, smiling.

"It's beautiful," she said, more of a sigh, exactly like a birthday girl should do. She wanted to say more, wanted to tell him why it meant so much to her, but she wasn't sure exactly where the line was tonight.

"You can put it on. If you want. If you like it," he said awkwardly.

With nervous fingers she lifted out the necklace, and tried to finesse the clasp, but he was watching her, and her fingers felt clumsy.

"Do you need help?"

"Do you mind?" she asked politely.

"No. Not at all," he said. He walked behind her, his hands at her neck, lifting her hair. The necklace settled into place, exactly as if it belonged there, and his fingers lingered, exactly as if they belonged there, until the waiter interrupted, and Daniel returned to his seat, exactly as if he belonged there.

"Thank you," she said, her fingers going to the necklace every few moments, feeling the fragile chain, afraid she would break it somehow.

"Anytime," he told her, and Daniel didn't say things he didn't mean, didn't do looks that he didn't mean, either, and she smiled nervously. Warm and scared, all at the same time.

After dinner, Daniel took her to a nightclub downtown. Not a loud place, but old-fashioned, quiet, with lots of dark corners for couples to be alone. A pianist accompanied a female singer with a deep, throaty voice.

He ordered a bottle of wine, and they spent the time reviewing the audit, but as he was talking, his fingers crept across the table, brushing hers, lightly once, and then, taking her hand. She knew he liked touching her, she knew he fought very hard not to and she loved those times when he couldn't help himself.

A shadow appeared over their table, a couple, cute and sparkling, and full of zest.

"Daniel?"

The fingers, so desperately holding on to hers, jerked away as if they'd been burned.

*Okay.*

Daniel stuck the burned hand under the table. "What are you doing out?" he asked. "I thought you had kids. I heard that killed a social life."

The man laughed. "They're at home with the babysitter. It's our tenth anniversary. I promised Lara it was date night."

Lara laughed, grabbing her husband's hand. "It happens so rarely now. Who is this?" she asked, forcing the introduction.

Daniel nodded in her direction. "This is Catherine. Catherine, this is Lara and Eric Dowling."

Nothing more. Not "my date," "my friend," "my lover," not even "the granddaughter of my client." So many labels to choose from, and he chose none, which was a choice in and of itself.

Lara looked at her, curiously, and Catherine wondered if they were comparing her to Michelle.

Catherine put her fingers to the diamond teardrop at her throat, wanting to tell Lara that Daniel had given it to her, just tonight, for her birthday, but then Lara would look at her strangely, wondering what insecurities had prompted that, so Catherine held her tongue.

"Still working downtown?" asked Eric.

"I am," answered Daniel, not saying anything more, not asking anything more.

Lara tugged at her husband's arm. "It was good to see you. Catherine," she said politely, and then they both walked away. Catherine looked at Daniel, who was studiously not looking at Eric and Lara. His mouth was tight and his eyes were hollow again.

"Would you like to dance?" he asked her.

She wasn't sure that dancing was the right answer, but she nodded and went into his arms, and there she could forget about labels and rules and trying to discover whether or not lines were being crossed.

"We used to go out with them," he said, by way of explanation.

"I figured that one out," she said, and his hand slid around her waist, curling there, and she knew he wanted her. No matter what label he picked or didn't pick, she knew that he wanted *her*. Catherine reached under his jacket, touching his back, and closed her eyes.

"They always were a little pretentious. Michelle used to make fun of them behind their backs. I told her it wasn't nice to do that, but I'd laugh anyway, because it was true. And they were good people. They just had flaws."

It was the longest speech he'd ever made about his wife, and Catherine was glad he'd told her something human about her. Catherine so desperately wanted to like this ghost of a woman who stood in between them.

As she danced there with him, moving in slow circles, as the music soothed her, as the smell of sandalwood reassured her, Catherine floated away from all those past lives and past friends.

This was their first. Their first dance and she knew she could dance with him again and again. She leaned her head against his shoulder, wondering if there was another deltoid-scapula combination so well-designed to fit her.

Not a chance. This one shoulder was pretty much it.

This broken man with the sorrowful eyes and a grin so long out of practice. This man who made love as if his life depended on it, who curled into her afterward as if his life depended on it.

Could people fall in love twice? She was betting her heart that the answer was yes, and yet, at the same time, she knew that she wouldn't ever feel like this again. The music cast a spell—soft, soulful and designed for people in love. She felt his mouth on her cheek, and she knew he was falling under the same spell that she was.

"Happy birthday," he whispered, kissing her lips, and she forgot about Lara and Eric and Michelle and everyone else. Right now, it was only Catherine and Daniel and the music, and that was all right with her.

# 14

IT WAS FOUR O'CLOCK in the morning, and a sane man would be asleep. Not Daniel. The knot keeping his sanity together was slowly slipping loose. He was getting used to walking around without his ring. At first, he didn't like the way Catherine's eyes would slip over to his left hand, as if it were some sort of test he was failing. Now, the mark of pale skin on his finger was disappearing from view, almost as if it had never existed at all.

*Dammit.*

He looked at Catherine. The birthday girl was sacked out, oblivious to the scary workings of his inner mind.

Catherine, who really loved her birthdays. He shook his head. Who knew? All she wanted was one day of pure, unadulterated happiness. Daniel completely understood that, and tonight he had taken her on an official date.

Before now, he could justify those dinners with Catherine, but not tonight. Tonight was all flowers and romance and bright gold jewelry.

Actually, if he wanted to do right by her, he'd just walk away from her. They'd found exactly zero evidence to support her claim that Charles Montefiore wasn't cooking the books to line his own pockets. It probably wouldn't be long before she wasn't talking to him, anyway. If he walked away now, that'd make her life easier, make his conscience clearer and make everything so simple, exactly like it was before.

But he couldn't walk away, they couldn't drag him away. He was bound to her in ways that he wasn't going to put under a microscope. He liked having her to talk to, he liked watching television with her and knowing she was there, he liked waking up with her and reaching out and knowing she was there.

Daniel liked being happy.

At some point, he should invite her to his apartment, but that felt weird in so many ways. Too many ways to count. There were pictures there…

Oh, man.

Why was he sitting up at four o'clock, staring at the woman half-buried under the covers, thinking about being happy when he should be contemplating the box of pictures stored in the back of his closet? The pictures that he had no place for, but it seemed stupid to take them back to the storage depot.

So where was he supposed to put them? On the walls? God, no. That would send Sean and Gabe over the edge. He didn't feel right about keeping them hidden in the closet, either. He looked outside, noted the sun would be coming up soon and he should leave, even though it was Saturday and was there any crime in sleeping late on the weekend?

After all, he wasn't solving the problem with the pictures tonight. Not enough time. Would there ever be enough time? Catherine's arm reached out, searching for him.

Nope. There was never going to be enough time. That was the way life was.

Daniel lay down and pulled her close, until she woke, soft and sleepy and so alive.

THE HOME OF Brianna Taylor Kelley was one of the old stately town houses along Central Park. Catherine was curious about the woman behind the ring, and Daniel seemed eager to put it behind him.

Last night, they had passed some milestone, and when he walked with her today, he held her hand as if they belonged together. Oh, hope was a troubling thing, but Catherine was still caught up in her own post-birthday glow, triggered by a post-birthday shower with Daniel that had brought him to his knees—an expression that could be interpreted in many different ways, all of them good.

A butler led them into the main room on the first floor, and Catherine's mind went straight into appraisal mode because Ms. Kelley's place was a gold mine, and she wondered if her grandfather knew. There were two beautiful matching Sevres presentation vases, sitting on the Louis XVI table in the corner that was probably George Jacob, or a really good imitator, and could easily bring in six figures. The carpet was Aubusson, circa 1750 or 1760. One of the paintings on the wall was an actual Gainsborough, a portrait of a young woman with blushing cheeks and love in her eyes. Catherine had always believed that it was a particular talent of the famed artist to bring that much happiness to his subjects. Earlier, when she'd looked in the mirror, she saw the blushing cheeks and the love in her own eyes.

"You like my things?"

Catherine looked up at the sound of the elegant voice, which perfectly matched the older woman's appearance—graceful white hair, an innate sense of style that even Sybil would have coveted. Ms. Kelley's smile was genuine, and she led them over to the giltwood love seat with thin Regency-style legs. Her mother loved such things, and Catherine eyed the carving on the legs to admire the craftsmanship and the exquisite condition. She glanced over, and noticed Daniel eyeing the legs as if he were afraid he would break it.

"I think I'll stand, if it's all right with you, ma'am," he told her politely. "I don't think this will take long. We found a ring that I believe belongs to you." He held it out, and placed it in Ms. Kelley's palm, and she welled up with tears.

"Where did you find this?"

Daniel smiled. "We own a bar. O'Sullivan's. When my brother tore down one of the walls, he found it."

"O'Sullivans. And you tracked it to me?" she said, her eyes staring at the ring.

"Yes, ma'am."

"It is yours?" asked Catherine.

"Oh, yes. The SCH is Samuel Coleridge Hollowell. He was named after the poet, but no relation. His mother simply loved the poetry of Robert Browning, but always confused the man with Samuel Coleridge and so Samuel ended up Samuel instead of Robert."

Catherine was intrigued. "Were you engaged to him at one time?"

She slipped the ring on her finger, holding up her hand to the light like a young girl. "We were married."

"Married?" Daniel sat down next to Catherine. "How did the ring end up at O'Sullivan's?"

Ms. Kelley, or rather Mrs. Hollowell, shook her head. "Samuel was a fireman for the City, just like his father and his grandfather. So big and strapping…and heroic." Her smile was full of misty memories. "That was my Samuel. Whenever there was a fire, he was the first one there. It was a fire that killed him. We'd only been married a year, but I felt as if I'd loved him forever. We were supposed to be together longer than that."

"I'm sorry. I know it was painful," Daniel said, and Catherine avoided looking at him. She didn't need to; the sorrow was apparent in his voice.

The old woman studied the ring in her palm. "There are some times that I almost forget, but I don't want to forget. We had so many good days, but not enough good days."

The room chilled, and Catherine rubbed at the goose bumps on her arm. There was a ghost in the room. Maybe two.

*Please let this conversation end soon.*

"You didn't remarry, did you?"

"No. Everyone wants to replace things, replace people, but this house is filled with irreplaceable things, and Samuel was irreplaceable, as well."

At that, Daniel stayed quiet. Catherine knew he'd found his answer.

"Where was the fire?" she asked, needing to change the subject. "How did the ring get from the fire to the bar?"

Ms. Kelley looked at her with kind eyes. "It was on Tenth Avenue."

"That's right near the bar," Daniel explained.

"There was an explosion."

"I'm so sorry," said Catherine, and she was. It wasn't fair that people had to hurt, that people had to lose the ones they loved. It wasn't fair at all. It wasn't fair to Ms. Kelley, it wasn't fair to Daniel and it wasn't fair to Catherine, either.

"We should go," said Daniel, rising to his feet. He looked at Catherine, nearly a smile. Not quite. It was never going to be quite enough.

"Of course. Thank you for the ring. I should give you a reward."

Daniel waved it off. "No, please."

She put the ring back on her hand and it still fit. Sixty years later and it still fit perfectly.

Daniel turneed pale, and Catherine scrubbed at the goose bumps again. It didn't matter how hard she tried; some things wouldn't go away.

THAT NIGHT, Daniel worked at Prime. He reconciled four months' worth of inventory, created budgetary projections into the year 2020 and analyzed the tax code of New York City, just in case.

Anything was better than thinking about this afternoon.

Sean came downstairs at around midnight, and no matter how hard Daniel tried to blend into the woodwork, he found him. That was the trouble with the storage room/office/basement. A man could run, but he really couldn't hide.

"Why are you still here? You should be gone."

"Catching up," answered Daniel. "I thought I'd make up for some time that I've missed."

"You dumped her, didn't you? We never even met her, but you couldn't handle it, could you?"

"Sean, don't you have a job upstairs?"

"Cain's up there. So is Gabe. So is Tessa. I'm fine." He pulled up a beer case and sat down, folding his arms across his chest. "Let's chat."

Daniel swore under his breath. "What do you want to know?" It was after midnight. He was extremely tired. He wanted to go see Catherine, but a man didn't show up at a woman's apartment at this time if he respected her at all, and besides, this afternoon had spooked him in a big way. If a seventy-year-old woman could live her life with one love, why couldn't Daniel?

"Let's start with the basic facts. Name."

"Catherine."

"Last name."

Daniel stayed silent.

"Okay. Next question. Where did you meet her?"

"None of your business."

"Fair enough. Next question. Did you dump her?"

"No."

"Then what the hell is wrong with you? Go home. Go be with her. Work some of that tension off."

"It's after midnight, Sean."

"So?"

Daniel looked up at the ceiling, as if white plaster could help him understand his brother's mind. "I don't show up at anybody's door this late."

"But you're not broken up. Right?"

"Yeah."

"What are you going to do next week?"

"I don't know, and I don't think it concerns you." Actually, Monday was Labor Day, and he was thinking about taking Catherine out to the Hamptons again. That'd be nice, although the traffic would be killer.

"Do you know what next Saturday is?"

Then it dawned on Daniel that Sean wasn't talking about Labor Day. He was talking about September eleventh.

Daniel swore again.

"Keep her, Daniel. If she can make you forget that god-damned day, then I don't care who she is or what she looks like."

"I hadn't forgotten," snapped Daniel. Because he hadn't. "It doesn't matter what I do. She's not going to like me very much in a couple weeks."

"Why not? She got this far with you. Who knows, she must have figured you out. You're not that complicated, Daniel. Don't flatter yourself."

"It's something else."

Sean sighed and stood up. Daniel heard Gabe's feet on the stairs. Wonderful.

"Sean, get your ass upstairs." Gabe looked at Daniel, surprised. "Why are you still here?"

"Does everyone forget I work here?"

"Not that much," answered Gabe. "Thanks for tracking down the ring lady."

"It wasn't a big deal."

Then Gabe turned to Sean, and turned back to Daniel. "What are you guys talking about so late?"

"Nothing," replied Daniel. And Gabe studied him suspiciously

"Tessa's ass," quipped Sean, which effectively got Daniel off the hook. He looked at Sean and nearly smiled. Nearly. Sean continued, "I tried to tell him that I didn't want to hear about it, I think it's quasi-creepy, eyeing your brother's girlfriend, but Daniel… It's the quiet ones you have to worry about. You wouldn't believe how many psychos are out there, never saying a word—"

"That's enough, Sean," interrupted Daniel.

"You can go home," said Gabe. "I don't want you looking at Tessa's ass, thank you very much. Go find a girlfriend of your own."

"I'm out of here," said Daniel, saving the files and packing his things away. Weirdly enough, he felt better. Not better enough to knock on Catherine's door, but he'd see her tomorrow. Early in the morning. Maybe she'd like breakfast. Scratch that. He'd been trying to wean off the food thing. Man, this date stuff was difficult.

He looked at his brothers and smiled.

Family. Not too shabby. Not too shabby at all.

CATHERINE WAS JUST waking up when she heard the buzzer at her door. She threw on a robe and pressed the button. "Daniel O'Sullivan's here, Miss Montefiore."

Catherine checked her clock. It was eight in the morning on Sunday. Did he never sleep? She looked down at her nightshirt and flannel boxers and huffed. This was so not fair. A miracle worker, she was not. Two seconds later, he was at her door. Catherine let him in, gazing wistfully at his jeans and white button-down, all neatly pressed. "Come on in."

"I'm sorry. I shouldn't have come so early." He didn't look sorry. He looked perky. And eager. And wide-awake. She, on the other hand, was a sleepy schlub.

"Is something wrong?' she asked, dragging a hand through her hair and finding a few tangles in the back.

"Oh, no. I knew you were anxious to work on the archives…."

"Uh, yeah."

"I can come back later. I'm sorry."

She waggled a finger at him. "Don't you start with the apologies. Let me go make some coffee. Wake up. Maybe get cleaned up. How do you do this?"

He noticed her portfolio lying open on the side table. "Do you mind if I look?"

Catherine blushed, but decided that, since the man had seen her naked, she shouldn't be shy about her art. Slowly, she nodded. "Don't tell me if they suck."

Daniel pulled out the sketches carefully and stared.

So, she had to ask. "What do you think?"

"I don't think they suck. I think they're very good. Better than very good. Excellent. Tons better than some of that crap at MoMA. I just don't get the whole modern art thing."

Catherine shrugged. "It's an acquired taste."

He looked at one, twisting the paper. "Is this me?"

Catherine slipped it out of his hands. "No."

He looked at her again. "Who else are you drawing?"

"Most of what I do is sketching from a sculpture or a painting. I'm not big on asking strange men to sit nude for me." She smiled.

"It was kind of fun."

"So you'd do it again…." she said, trailing off in a leading voice.

"Under duress, only."

"Thank you," she said.

"Can I have one? Not the ones of me. That would be weird and Sean, or even Gabe—they wouldn't understand. But this one. The lady sitting in the chair, looking out the window. That's really nice. If you don't mind, I mean, if you do, it's okay, and I'd completely understand."

"No, you can take it. I'd love for you to take it. You can even take two if you'd like. I can share."

He met her eyes for a moment and she realized what they'd done. They had shared. She grinned at him, possibly goofy in her Killers T-shirt and plaid flannel boxers, with a hulking tangle in the back of her hair, but she liked this.

"I missed you last night," he told her. More sharing, definitely more sharing. Oh, she was really starting to like this sharing stuff.

"I did, too," she said, and then he kissed her. She truly did love kissing him; it was like floating. She could feel his hips pressing against her, sure, steady and completely stimulating.

He lifted his head. "Coffee? Or shower?"

Catherine didn't hesitate. "Shower."

"I could wash your back," he offered, because he was that sort of man.

"I thought you'd never ask."

Two hours later, and they were draped across her bed, and Daniel was looking at her sketches. "These are really good. Have you shown them to your grandfather, or mother or somebody that knows about art?"

"Nah. They're aware I play around at this, but I get nervous."

He stretched, muscles bunching along the line of his torso, and Catherine thought she'd never crave cupcakes again. He was so much tastier, and zero calories, zero fat, too. "You shouldn't be nervous," he said, completely oblivious to her ogling.

"Tell that to my stomach," she said, just as the phone in her apartment rang. Reluctantly, she undraped herself from Daniel and the bed. "That's probably my mother. She's that way when she's in New York."

It wasn't her mother. It was Sybil.

"Okay, it's Labor Day weekend. What are we doing? I'm thinking, like, maybe the Shore, or maybe Jones Beach. The Hamptons possibly. What say you?"

"Oh, uh…" And Catherine looked at Daniel. "I think I'm going to work today," she said, with a question in her eyes. He nodded.

"So, you heard."

"Heard what?"

"About Charles's e-mails to Chadwick. There was a presentation to the board last Monday. I wasn't sure if you knew or not. The final audit report is next Friday. You didn't seem, like, bummed or anything, and I didn't want to depress you, but I still don't believe it about your grandfather."

"Thank you for not telling me," muttered Catherine. She watched as Daniel undraped himself from her bed, and pulled on his jeans, carefully avoiding her gaze.

"Sorry, Catherine. If you need me. I'm here."

"Thanks," said Catherine, and then she hung up, wishing she wasn't naked. It wasn't right that she should be decimated like this, and be caught without clothes. She stalked into her bedroom and wrapped a robe around her like an avenging goddess coming down to smite the one mortal who was so going to pay for this.

"Why didn't you tell me?" she asked.

He stood, taller than her, broader than her, but those things didn't matter. He should have told her. "I couldn't."

"What? Now your duty calls? Some idiotic code that lets you sleep with the subject in question, lets her help you with your work, but then withhold one key piece of evidence?"

"I knew you'd be mad. I didn't want to tell you. I didn't want to hurt you."

Catherine paced around the room, robe flying in her wake, and it didn't help that the sheets were well-tousled, and that he smelled like sandalwood and sex. "Well, it's too freaking late for that."

"I'm sorry."

"When did you find these e-mails?" She sat down on the bed, he sat beside her, reaching for her, and she shook his hand away. Not now. Not now.

"They were there almost from the first. Steve, your IT manager, he got me into the system, and they weren't hard to find."

"My grandfather hates e-mail."

"A lot of people do."

She looked at him flatly. "He doesn't use it."

"Apparently he did, more than once."

"Are you also aware that my grandfather's user ID and password are pasted behind the calendar on his desk, and most employees at Montefiore know exactly what they are?"

His brows came together in a V. "That doesn't sound very secure."

"We're an auction house. Not a bank. Security is spent on the art, not the e-mail system."

"You don't think he sent it."

She popped up, mad enough to hit. "Duh."

"So who would, Catherine?"

"Someone who wants to make my grandfather look bad," she answered, frowning.

"This is coming from inside the company. Not outside."

"Then it's an employee with a grudge."

"Maybe somebody is trying to make some extra money," he said carefully.

"Not enough people directly make money from padding the profits."

"Your grandfather, your mother and you."

She froze. Stared. Then pointed to the door. "You can get out now."

"I don't believe it," he said, his eyes no longer impassive.

"But you're setting my grandfather up for a fall, even though you think he didn't do anything? What are you going to say on Friday?"

"I'll report the facts as I've found them. I'm an auditor, Catherine. Nothing more."

Catherine resumed her pacing, thinking, trying to figure out what to do.

"I'm something more," she answered.

"Yes, you are," he said, and just like that he'd thrown her another curveball. Surely, she didn't need to be swinging at curveballs at the moment.

"We're going to do something. We will go through every box until I find something, anything that proves my grandfather is innocent."

"Okay," he told her, but it was there on his face. He didn't believe her grandfather was innocent. Daniel was merely humoring her.

Screw that.

"I'll do it myself."

"I want to help you," he insisted.

"I don't need someone who's trying to send my grandfather to jail."

"I'm not the cops, Catherine."

"Save it, Daniel. Why don't you go? I have a long day."

"No." He shrugged slowly, and his jaw got stubborn. She had seen that look before when he was working, but she'd never seen it directed at her.

"What do you mean, 'no'?"

"I'm not leaving. Not like this. You need me."

"I do not."

"How many audits have you done, Catherine?" he asked, putting on his shirt.

She glared, since she didn't want him to be right. She didn't want to need him. Not with the audit. Not with anything.

"Go get dressed."

"I will not," she said, still mad.

"You're going to Montefiore like that? It's cute, but...I wouldn't."

She didn't want to smile. She didn't want to smile. She didn't want to smile.

She smiled. A tiny twitch on the right-hand side. He saw it.

Bastard.

God, she loved this man.

"What if there isn't anything to find?" asked Catherine, thinking the unthinkable.

He took her into his arms and held her, strong, sure and satisfied. "We don't know that. If somebody is setting up your grandfather, they'll have made a mistake. All crooks make them eventually."

THE MONTEFIORE offices were mostly empty. All but a few die-hard employees had taken the holiday weekend off. On Sunday, she and Daniel worked long into the night, and had found another thirty invoices that didn't match, but nothing more.

Catherine didn't want to think her grandfather had done anything, but late at night, when her eyes hurt from the endless numbers, the doubts would creep in.

"I don't think he sent the e-mails, Daniel. Grandfather is a total Luddite. He wouldn't do it."

Daniel put aside the invoice he was working on. "So we check out who else could have sent it."

"Everybody. Anybody."

"Maybe we talk to IT, then. I assumed it was legit. If not, maybe they were careless enough to use their own computer and not your grandfather's."

"You can check that out?"

"Sure. We'll call Steve and see if he'll let us into the communications systems."

"I thought you just did audits."

"I'm a man of many talents," answered Daniel with a weak smile. "Besides, it's pretty standard stuff."

She stared at him, nervous, and felt her heart turn over—twice. She wanted to tell him, but she didn't. More sharing. And this wasn't the petty-birthday sharing. This was the big stuff. Nope, not there yet.

"You're tired?" he asked.

"Yeah," she said.

He rose, pulled her by the hand. "Tomorrow's another day. Let's go home."

THE NEXT MORNING was much of the same, and Catherine felt the tension eating away inside her every second that passed, which moved her closer to Friday.

"Have you heard from Steve?" she asked, for the third time, even though Daniel was sitting only a foot away from her, and his cell would ring, not vibrate, so she knew exactly when he received a phone call. Still, the anxiety was killing her.

His cell rang and Catherine popped out of her seat.

"O'Sullivan.

"Yeah. Yeah. Yeah."

If he said "yeah" one more time, Catherine was going to hit him.

Daniel hung up. "That was Steve. He was relaxing at home, but he'll be here in an hour."

Catherine looked at her watch. "An hour? That long?"

He came over, and sat on the edge of the table next to her. "It's going to be okay, Catherine."

"You don't know that. There's nothing but two sets of invoices and we don't even know which ones are correct."

"Sure we do."

She stared at him curiously. "What did you find out?"

"The originals are correct. I did some checking. Your customers have records of what they were charged. We were discreet, and yes, it's the originals that are correct. Not the digital copies. Those have been doctored."

"So what does that prove?"

"I'm not sure."

"What if there's nothing in the computer e-mail log as well?"

"I don't know, but don't think like that."

"I hate this."

"I'm sorry," he said, and took her hand. "I wish I could make it go away for you."

And then she felt bad because she was acting like such a child, but she'd never shown grace under pressure. All this building and building, until she felt as if she was ready to explode.

"You want a break?" he asked with courteous concern.

"We should work," she said, pushing back her hair, and his gaze tracked the agitated rise and fall of her breasts. All that pressure…

"There's an hour before Steve's here," he noted, not so much courteous concern.

"We can get a lot done in an hour." She used her mother's appraisal stare on him. And it worked.

He started to smile, his eyes dark, and he took her by the shirt, pulled her closer and kissed her full on the mouth. All that pressure, all that glorious pressure. Catherine unashamedly scooched into him because she now understood why she wasn't grace under pressure. She was horny under pressure, which put a completely different spin on things, and apparently Daniel knew exactly how to handle it, how to handle her. His hands held her cheeks, and she yanked his pressed shirt free from his pants.

"I'm sorry. Am I interrupting?"

Catherine jumped off the table, and Daniel flew to the other side of the room.

Foster Sykes looked at the two of them, and Catherine felt a blush on her cheeks. "No. Not interrupting. Not interrupting at all."

"What did you need?" asked Daniel, calm, cool. Now *that* was grace under pressure.

"I saw the lights on, thought I'd check and see how it was going. If you needed anything, but I guess not."

"Steve Keating is coming in to go over some of the logs in the e-mail servers," Daniel explained.

"Good, good," said Foster. "I'm sorry. I honestly didn't know. I'll go now."

After he disappeared from the room, Catherine sighed. "Okay, back to work."

Daniel nodded. "Yeah."

Steve showed up an hour later, exactly as he'd promised. He'd been the resident IT geek at Montefiore for almost ten years, and he looked the part with a baby face and a two-game-a-day Xbox habit. Although they were from completely different planets, Catherine thought he was nice.

"What do you need?" he asked, dressed in the requisite surfer shorts and flip-flops, looking as if he'd just come from the beach.

"Thanks for coming in on the holiday," Daniel told him, shaking his head. "I'm sorry to take you away from the water."

"I was playing Halo Three."

"Oh. Well. So, I was thinking about checking over the e-mail server logs. What sort of tracking do you have in-house?"

They got into a detailed conversation about services, permissions and event logs that went completely over Catherine's head.

"Do you mind if I take a look at the logs?" asked Daniel and Steve laughed.

"Not a problem, dude. Boring, though." He badged them into the server room, and the temperature dropped forty degrees.

"It's very cold here," she said, rubbing her hands together.

"You get used to it," answered Steve. He went over to one of the racks of machines, pulled out a keyboard and went to work. "Here's what you need."

Daniel stood behind him, watching. "What else is on the box?"

"Pretty much everything. Phones, e-mail, and then we back-up to tape over there."

Daniel nodded wisely, and looked at Catherine, who nodded wisely, too.

"Here are the days you're looking for," said Steve and he sent the file to the printer.

"You don't mind if I take this?" asked Daniel.

"Go ahead. No secrets here," he said.

Four hours later, they had looked over twelve months' worth of e-mail logs, Catherine reading over Daniel's shoulder.

"There's nothing here, is there?"

"Nope. The e-mails between Montefiore and Chadwick's came from your grandfather's computer."

She tugged her hand through her hair. "What's going to happen to the company?"

"I don't know," said Daniel with a shrug. "Let's get out of here."

"But maybe there's something—"

He shook his head. "Steve gave me an idea. Let's go to the beach."

THE HARDEST PART of being back at the beach house was how completely different Daniel was this time. He was working so hard to make her forget the audit that it wasn't like before when they were two strangers awkwardly getting to know each other.

Now, he was acting as if they were two lovers.

By the time they reached the Hamptons it was almost dark, but Catherine didn't care. Dark was wonderful, dark was romantic, dark made her not remember.

She brought out a bottle of wine, and they sat on the deck, listening to the distant roar of the waves. Constant, comforting.

"It's so nice out here. I always took it for granted."

He stared down the long expanse of beach. "I think we're the only two people on Long Island at the *end* of Labor Day."

She clinked her glass to his. "Beats all the traffic."

He reached out, touched her hair. "You look better."

"I feel better."

"Catherine," he began, but she put a finger to his lips because she didn't want him to say anything. She wanted her perfect night at the beach with the man she loved. The one she deserved. The one that he deserved. She took him by the hand and led him into the house, into her bed. He cupped her face in his hands and kissed her tenderly, as if she were the rarest sort of porcelain. He slid the shorts from her legs, and she wasn't nervous or shy. She drew the shirt from his shoulders and he watched her with purposeful eyes. They had come so far in such a short time.

His hands were gentle and reverent, tracing her curves, caressing her skin, and she smiled at him, smiled at the dulcet moonlight that drifted in through the window like music. Tonight he was thorough in his attentions, whispering how beautiful she was, how much it meant to him to be with her.

He savored the arch of her neck until she was limp, laving at her breasts until she bent into him like a willow, and farther down, teasing between her thighs until her muscles trembled with delight. Everything was slow tonight, the urgency gone, and his mouth skimmed up her body, taking her lips again. Lingering, loving. She nearly told him. The words were there on

her tongue, ready to be delivered in his ear, against his skin
but she held back because this was her secret, not to be shared
He slid inside her, filling her, their bodies moved together, each
stroke blending into the next with a beauty that no artist would
ever re-create.

Catherine's eyes drifted down because she didn't want him
to know, but he took her chin between his fingers and made her
look. So much in his eyes. Tenderness and passion, and everything that a woman could ever want.

Everything except love.

# 15

DANIEL MADE IT BACK to his apartment before first light. He'd just stepped out of the shower when the phone rang.

"Daniel, Timothy Lockhart here."

*His boss.* "Yes, sir."

"Can you come downtown? We need to talk."

DANIEL WALKED OUT of Lockhart's office, eyes carefully ahead. Okay, he hadn't been fired, although if Lockhart had been a stickler, he was within his rights.

*Having an affair with someone closely connected to the client.*

Is that what he'd been reduced to? Somehow it was worse hearing the words from Michelle's boss. Michelle and Daniel had had dinner with Timothy and his wife. Daniel had sent his son a present when he graduated from Harvard. Hell, he was still on their Christmas list.

Probably not anymore.

He kept trying to put his past life behind him, but he couldn't. Everywhere he looked, everyone he knew was there to remind him that you could never escape from the past.

It wasn't fair to Catherine, and it wasn't fair to Michelle. It probably wasn't even fair to himself.

He'd been pretending too long. Pretending that he could sleep with Catherine and that it would turn out fine. Oh, yeah, it'd completely turned out fine.

They were bringing in a new auditor, who would deliver Daniel's report exactly as he'd written it. There was a pattern of collusion with Chadwick's, and all evidence indicated that Charles Montefiore was the man involved.

No, time to face the facts and deal.

DANIEL CALLED and wanted Catherine to meet him at the gazebo in the park. There was extra gravity in his voice. Always before he'd been so careful not to worry her, to make her feel secure, but not now.

"What's wrong?" she asked.

"I'll tell you when I get there," he answered, not bothering to deny there was something wrong.

The wind was kicking up. A front blowing in and the air was chilled and cold. When he got there, he didn't wait to tell her.

"I got pulled from the audit."

"For what?"

"Sleeping with you."

Okay, that explained the serious tone. "Are you in trouble?"

"No. It goes on my record, and it's a black mark, but they don't like advertising their failures, so they'll keep it quiet."

His face looked so hard and lined. Like it had that first day at the beach, and she at once knew what was wrong. The loneliness was back. "I'm sorry."

"You didn't do anything wrong, Catherine. It was my screwup."

"How did they know?"

"A member of the board got an anonymous phone call saying my credibility had been compromised because of our relationship."

"I'm sorry," she said. Foster Sykes must have spoken to someone.

"Stop apologizing, Catherine. It's not a big problem," he said, with eyes that said there was a bigger problem looming.

"What else?"

"They're going to use my report."

"What's in that report, Daniel?" she asked quietly.

"Nothing that will make you happy. I'm sorry."

"I thought you were thorough and detailed."

"I am. Sometimes it doesn't change the outcome."

He sat down on the bench across from her, rubbing his hands back and forth on his expensive wool pants. That was when she noticed the ring.

It was back.

"What else?" she asked, but she knew. This was it. There was no reason for them to see each other anymore. The temptation of blood-pumping, bedpost-shaking, hoo-haw-busting sexual experiences would be gone.

However, today she was going to make him say it because she knew he'd hate saying it, but she was mad, and vindictive, and all those boiling things that she'd never thought she'd think about herself before. Of course, she'd never been in love before, either.

"I haven't been realistic and it's hurt you, and I'm sorry. I thought I could do this. I thought I could have a relationship, but I can't. I've loved the time we had, and there's absolutely no other woman that I would want to be with other than you, but this limbo isn't fair to you, and I don't think I can move past it."

She looked at him, head high, and stared him right smack in the eyes until he was the one who had to look away.

"Aren't you going to say anything?" he asked.

"No," she said coolly, so coolly that she saw him wince. Then she stood to go.

There wasn't anything she could say, wasn't anything she could do. Deep down she had always known they'd end up like this. With a flourish, Catherine slung her faux Prada bag over her shoulder and heard the seams rip even farther apart. Because at the most personal of levels there were some things that just couldn't be faked no matter what.

# 16

WEDNESDAY NIGHT poker was at Sean's apartment and Daniel wasn't saying much. He played his cards with more aggression than brains, and slammed shots with a lot more aggression than brains.

Gabe looked at him curiously. "This is new."

"No, this is old," he said, upping Gabe's twenty with another twenty, although there was absolutely nothing in his hand. But tonight he felt like throwing everything just for the hell of it.

Gabe counted his chips, then turned back to his brother. "No anonymous bars? I have to say, I like this better. I don't have to pick you up from strange parts unknown. You can even crash on Sean's couch and we don't have to go anywhere. Just dust you off in the morning and roll you out the door. So what's the plan for 9/11 this year? Yonkers? The Bronx, oh, that was a fun one, wasn't it? Putnam County? I don't even know how you got up there. How does a man without a car end up in Putnam County?"

"Why don't you lay off him, Gabe?"

This from Sean, who had never defended Daniel in his life. Later, when Daniel was approaching sobriety, he might appreciate it, but the alcohol was numbing him, and he wanted the numb. Comfortably numb.

"Why should I lay off him? He deserves it. You were right,

Sean, and I hate admitting it, but this time you are. Tough love. We've been enabling this, encouraging him to live every day like it's 9/10, like we're in some 9/11 time warp, and it never happened. Well, it's not right."

"I don't think this is a 9/11 problem," spoke Sean softly.

Daniel poured himself another shot. He and sour mash were old friends. Old, old friends. "Can we not talk as if I'm not here?" he said, toasting to nothing, and then pouring the drink down his throat.

"I'm not doing it," said Cain. "I'm only here to play cards. Maybe drink. This sounds like a family issue. Doesn't concern me."

"Thank you."

"Don't thank me. You're easier to beat when you've had a few. I like it."

Six shots later, and Daniel had dropped another two hundred to Sean, which was a humiliation in and of itself. When the bottle of whiskey was empty, he went into the kitchen to dig out another one, and Sean followed him there.

"Did you see Claudia?"

"She wanted some pictures," answered Daniel, knowing that would stop the conversation in its tracks. And it did.

"How's the audit coming?" asked Sean.

"Got a new assignment."

"Oh."

Gabe was frowning, and Daniel blinked. Gabe was here? Oh, yeah. "Where was your last assignment?" he asked.

"Auction house," Sean replied.

Daniel frowned. He poured another shot and Sean took it away from him.

"That's what this is about?" Gabe asked.

"That's what what is about?" mimicked Daniel. He didn't want to talk about Catherine. He didn't want to talk about the long nights when he was going to bed alone again. He didn't want to talk about going back to frozen dinners, or to the months by himself, or the single load of laundry he sent out each week.

Sean grimaced. "You're not seeing her anymore, are you?"

"Who?" he asked, stealing the shot glass.

"Transitional babe."

"She was not transitional babe," he said stubbornly.

"So why aren't you still seeing her? Sounds like you've transitioned out of her," Sean speculated while moving the shot glass out of Daniel's reach.

"Leave me alone," snapped Daniel as he took back the glass.

Sean knew when it was time to fold. "All right. I'll leave you alone. But Gabe's right. No more enabling. Tough love. Love you, man, but from now on, don't call me when you're stuck at some bar and can't find your way home. I'll look at the caller ID, know it's you and I'm not going to answer it."

Daniel blinked at his brother. Once, and then twice. There were fuzzy lines around Sean that weren't normally there, and he knew he needed to shake it off. "I need to go," he said.

"Where?" Sean's grimace grew more severe.

"It's an emergency."

"What sort of emergency?" Gabe jumped in.

"Accounting. Bad. Very bad. What's today?"

"September eighth," Gabe told him.

"No, no, not the date. The day. Monday, Tuesday, Wednesday…"

"It's Wednesday."

"Good. It's not Friday. I've still got time."

"What's Friday, Daniel?" Sean called, but Daniel was already halfway out the door.

IT WAS NEARLY MIDNIGHT when the buzzer rang. It was Daniel on the other end of the intercom.

"Can you get me in the building?" he said, his voice unsteady

"My building?"

"Montefiore's. I need to get inside there."

"Now?"

"It's important," he said, and she realized he'd been drinking. Wow, broke up with her, and now driven to drink. She
shouldn't feel so happy about that, but she was, and she hoped
he'd had a miserable hangover, too.

"Why?"

"It's Wednesday."

"I know it's Wednesday, Daniel. Why do you want inside
the building?"

"Do you want your grandfather cleared?"

She looked at the intercom, and glared. "Yeah."

"He's really a phone guy?"

Ah, there was a method to the drunken madness. She just
had to follow it. "He hates computers. He won't use them.
Trust me. This is a man with an ink-and-pen set on his desk and
it's not there for show."

"Listen, can you get me into the building tonight? When
Steve got me into the e-mail system, I could see the phone
logs, too. We're in the digital age. It's not as good as the
e-mail trail, but I think we might be able to figure something
out."

"Why are you doing this?" she asked finally, wishing she
could look at his face, see his eyes, see what he was thinking
but all she had was six inches of metal with one white plastic
button. It didn't show nearly enough.

"Because I'm a thorough, detailed jerk, that's why."

Catherine's finger shot to the intercom. Juvenile, yes, but ca-
thartic, as well. "Okay."

Ten minutes later, she was downstairs, dressed, and they
were walking the four blocks up Amsterdam to Montefiore's

Daniel didn't look nearly as well-pressed as he normally did. He was wearing a tie, barely. One shirttail was out, but his eyes were focused and sure. Once they got inside, she bribed the security guard to get her into the server room, where they stood staring at the rack of machines for several moments.

"I don't know his password."

Daniel shot a loopy grin in her direction, and she hated how her heart thumped. This was the man who had just dumped her and was going to implicate her grandfather in a collusion scandal. There should be no heart-thumping, not even heart-blipping. She shouldn't feel anything for him at all.

"You would make a bad auditor," he said, and pulled out the keyboard drawer.

She watched as his fingers typed on the keys.

"How did you know that?"

"I watched him type it," admitted Daniel, and her heart thumped again. A definite thump. Definitely. What happened to cold and impassive? That she was prepared for. But drunk and heroic? The gods had no mercy. None.

He looked at the screen, frowned and started talking to himself.

"No, no, no, no, no, no, no, no, yup, no, no, no, no, no, no, no, yup, yup, no, no, no, no…oh, look at that…."

Catherine leaned in closer. "Look at what? What is that?"

"Chadwick's. Someone's been talking to Chadwick's."

"Who?"

"I don't know. Do you recognize the extension?"

"No. There are over a hundred employees here."

"Is it your grandfather's, your mother's or yours?"

"No, no and no."

"Good, good and better."

He shifted, a satisfied smile on his face. "There. Case closed," he said and walked out of the server room.

Catherine ran after him.

"Wait!"

Daniel turned.

"Where are you going?" she asked.

His smile faltered. "I don't know. Maybe the Bronx. Maybe Orange County. I haven't been there yet. I imagine they have pretty decent bars there. I should check it out."

"Why are you doing this?"

He stared at her as if she were a ghost. "Because I love you."

Then he walked off into the night.

AT 9:00 A.M. the next morning, Catherine called an emergency meeting in the break room.

"I need to talk."

"Oh, yeah, like, I bet you do," said Sybil. "I have to hear about your affair from the boardroom walls?"

"What affair?" gasped Brittany.

"With Daniel."

"Daniel?" asked Brittany. "Daniel? That Daniel? Oh. No. Way. An affair. Was he good?"

"I need help."

"I don't think so," said Sybil, pouring herself a cup of coffee. "I think if you wanted help, you would have said something, like when we got stuck in the purse stall on Canal Street."

Brittany took a step back and stared at Sybil. "You were on Canal Street? Okay. We need to talk. You two have been keeping secrets and this is so not fair. I'm part of this team."

"He told me he loved me." Catherine had been repeating the words to herself all night, but she needed to say them to someone else. It made them feel real.

"Great. Send me the wedding invitation," teased Sybil.

"He was drunk."

Brittany nodded. "Was he trying to get into your pants at the same time? Gets drunks, gets a little friendly, and suddenly, it's 'oh, I luuurvvee you. I want to slurp you up.' I hate that, because it's wrong. Really, really wrong. Was he trying to get into your pants?"

Catherine looked down at the floor. "Unfortunately, no."

"Really?" asked Sybil.

Catherine glared. "Hey, he was the one who found out that Steve was talking to Chadwick's, and setting up my grandfather."

"Guys, wait. I'm so totally lost here. Why was Steve talking to Chadwick's?" asked Brittany.

"Smithwick-Whyte was paying him," said Catherine.

"Smithwick-Whyte! Really?"

Sybil nodded. "They wanted the Drexel estate auction, but they were the long shot, so they set up both Chadwick's and Montefiore's to take a fall, leaving S and W to pick up the pieces. Steve was taking bribes and there was some VP at Chadwick's who was taking bribes and they were both fixing the system to make it look like there was collusion."

"Wow!"

"So what's next?" asked Sybil, Jimmy Choos tapping impatiently on the marble.

"Lunch. Lunch should be next."

"Are we going to hear everything about the affair?" asked Brittany. "You really have to share."

Catherine looked at Sybil, who was grinning mischievously and nodded. "Okay, I'll share."

DANIEL HAD FOUND the time to take Michelle's pictures to her mother. It wasn't easy sitting there, watching Claudia look at the images of her daughter with such love in her eyes, but Daniel did. As she went through them, she told him stories that he'd heard at least eight times before, but he always pretended as if it were the first time. Daniel was good at pretending.

Eventually, Claudia put the box away and turned her attention to him. "I haven't seen you this hollow-eyed in seven years. Maybe it's time for you to leave New York, not me."

So many times he had thought about leaving. Taking off for someplace new, trying to start over, but New York was his home. His brothers were here. It was all he had left. "No."

Claudia studied him carefully. Her eyes were the same blue as Michelle's, and he shifted uncomfortably. He didn't want his mother-in-law to know that he had been unfaithful to her daughter, but she did. "This isn't about Michelle."

He thought about lying to her, but what was the point? "No."

He looked at the ring on his hand and remembered the day that Michelle had put it on his finger. It wasn't supposed to come off.

"I made a promise to your daughter. I had our life so completely and carefully planned. It wasn't supposed to be so fucked. She didn't deserve it."

Claudia reached out and took his hand, wrapping her fingers around his palm. "She didn't deserve it, and neither did you. You can't live like this forever, Daniel. She wouldn't want you to."

"I thought you'd be mad. I know Michelle would be furious. She told me exactly what would happen if I ever cheated on her. She was very specific. I never thought that would be me. Ever."

Claudia looked at him, and he saw the gleam of tears in her eyes. "Michelle's gone now and I can't change that, and you can't change that. I wasn't supposed to bury a daughter, you weren't supposed to bury a wife, but we did. And you're too young for this. I love you, Daniel O'Sullivan. You are the son I always wanted, and I want you to be happy. Does this new girl make you happy?"

Daniel nodded. "I didn't think I could feel like this again. I had a hole inside me. It's gone."

"Then you need to be with her. Don't take happiness for granted. It doesn't happen enough. You'll have kids, right?"

"At the moment, I think she's mad at me."

"You need to fix that, and when you do have kids, will you bring them to see me? I want my grandchildren, and you're the only hope that I have."

"If you want," said Daniel, promising things that he had no business promising.

"I can see you with a little girl."

Daniel closed his eyes. He didn't want to think about families and kids and trips to the candy store and summer vacations at the beach. At one time, those thoughts had Michelle standing next to him, but now Michelle was gone, and the only woman he could imagine there was Catherine. "I don't know that I can do this."

"Don't wait too long, Daniel. I was married to my Bernard for forty-three years, and I wouldn't get married again because I was too old, too set in my ways. You're set in your ways, but you're not too old, Daniel."

"You're not going to move to Florida?"

"This is my home. I've lived here for sixty years and besides, I hate golf, and all that sun would be bad for my skin. There are memories here, good memories, and I don't want to lose them, but I can be happy, too."

"I think you could be happy."

"Bring me the grandkids, and I'll be happy."

Daniel stepped outside her door, and looked up to study the sky. It was a bright, shining September morning. He took the ring off his finger, brought it to his lips and then tucked it away.

It was time.

CATHERINE WAS ABOUT ready to leave work when her cell phone rang.

"I need to see you."

Daniel. She'd gotten used to hearing his voice, smelling his cologne, seeing him, touching him....

"Is it about the audit?" she asked carefully.

"No. I want you to come here, Catherine."

"Where is here?"

"Will you come to my apartment?"

She didn't want to go to his apartment. It was probably a shrine with thousands of pictures on the wall, little trinkets that had been given to him as wedding presents and a needlepoint announcement with wedding bells and pretty pink flowers, probably done by Michelle herself. "I don't know. You could come to my apartment instead. It'd be easier. It's closer."

They were excuses and he knew it. "Please. It's important."

Catherine straightened her spine. "Tell me where and I'll be there."

Forty-five minutes later, she was standing at his door, with a pulse that wouldn't slow down and the usual nervous stomach. He answered the door, well-pressed, smelling like sandalwood, and led her inside.

Catherine looked around.

Okay.

It was a typical Manhattan apartment. There were no burning candles, or needlepointed wedding announcements. The couch was brown leather, bacheloresque, but tasteful bacheloresque. It seemed spacious…sanitized, and then she saw the picture hanging in the corner. It wasn't a wedding picture, or a photograph of Michelle and Daniel together. It was her sketch. Framed, matted and looking as if it belonged there.

She walked over and looked at it, looked at her scrawled signature in the corner, and Catherine started to cry. She didn't like to cry around people. Crying was something private and personal, and implied ties, but the tears slid unchecked down her cheeks.

He came up close behind, almost touching her, but not quite. He even lifted his hands, but then forced them back down to his sides.

"I didn't mean to hurt you," he said, and she could tell where this was going. She wiped her face and headed for the door, but he caught her. This time, he did touch her.

"I didn't want to love you. I didn't want to love anybody. You didn't ask for anything, you didn't demand anything, you never took, only gave and then gave some more, and I was the one who was taking everything, bleeding you dry, and I knew it, too. But you didn't whine or complain. I think that's the reason I fell in love with you."

Catherine sniffed once. "You make me sound like a doormat."

He whacked himself on the forehead with his palm, but his eyes were soft. "I'm so bad at words. I think that's why I'm an accountant. Gabe and Sean, they can talk. Not me. Never could. You're no doormat, Catherine. You have no idea how strong you are, how talented you are, how special you are. But I do. I didn't expect it because you hide it so well from everybody, and you kept surprising me."

She took a step back, until there was a safe distance between them. "What are you doing?"

"I don't know what I'm doing, but I am tired of being alone, and I didn't know I was tired of being alone until I met you."

"Just me?"

"Yup. Just you. When I saw you on the beach, I knew I didn't have anything to be scared of. You were so much like me that it was easy. So quiet, so lonely, but you weren't going to be with just anyone. You had to find the exact right person, and thankfully I think it's me."

"I don't know," she said, because Catherine was smart and careful and wasn't going to be with just anyone.

"I love you, Catherine."

He was waiting for her to share, but these things he was talking about were serious and forever, and Catherine didn't take serious and forever lightly. She didn't think Daniel did, either, but she had been through so much with him, for him, because of him. She wasn't ready. Not yet.

"Why aren't you saying anything?" he asked, looking nervous.

"I'm not sure."

"About saying something, or about this?"

"About this."

"Will you try? Please, take a chance, Catherine. I deserve a chance. I know that now. I deserve a chance."

It surprised her that he expected her to give in so easily, but she'd learned some things since they'd been together. She was stronger. "Maybe this is temporary."

"Catherine, do you know me?"

"Yes."

"I don't think temporary is going to be my problem."

Okay, he was probably right there. But the list of bad possibilities went on. "I'm not Michelle."

"I know that."

"What if somebody comes along that's, you know, more like her?" Catherine asked, which was her polite way of saying that she wasn't some knockout in a Vera Wang gown, and her skirts would always hang a little off, and she would give up buttercream cupcakes for no man, so if he was going to take her, this was what he got.

"If I meet another woman like Michelle, I'll smile nicely and then go home and make love to the woman I love, and think how lucky I am to have someone like you who wants to be with someone like me."

And he believed it. He honestly believed that he was the lucky one. At which time, Catherine decided to admit that maybe, possibly, it was worth a try.

She went to him then. "We try," she said, clutching at the teardrop hanging from her neck.

His arms were outstretched. "Good."

She hugged him, awkwardly at first, because she was so scared. She didn't believe in many things, and although she believed in him, she wasn't quite ready to believe in them. But when he looked at her, she could swear that really was love in his eyes. When she spotted her picture on his wall, she thought...maybe.

And she gave herself up to him, gave him her heart, but still, she held back a little bit of her soul.

SHE CALLED IN SICK on Friday. She wasn't normally a person who called in sick, and thirty minutes later her mother called her cell, wanting to know what was wrong.

"I'm fine, Mom."

"Then why aren't you at work?"

"I'm taking a personal day."

"But you're not going to tell me what you're really doing, are you?"

Catherine looked over at Daniel and smiled. "I'm with Daniel, Mom. Everything is fine."

"Thank you, Catherine. Oh, and your grandfather wants you in his office first thing next week—seems he wants to expand your role at Montefiore's given your help with the audit. He thinks you're ready for the additional responsibility."

"Really?"

"Absolutely. He does love you, you know. And I love you, too, Catherine."

"Love you, Mom."

After she hung up, he reached out for her. "What do you want to do today?"

She didn't really want to do anything. She wanted to lie in his bed and watch the autumn sun play on his chest, and then watch her fingers play on his chest. "Could we stay here?" she asked. "I don't want to go out."

His smile started slow, and then grew. "You're not going to want to draw me again, are you?"

"Not today," she answered primly, when he took her into his arms. "That's tomorrow."

ON FRIDAY NIGHT, they went to Prime because he wanted her to see the bar, wanted her to meet his family. It was odd seeing the three brothers standing together. There were similarities, but there were a lot of differences, too. Gabe, with a ready smile, and Sean, who looked as if he was always ready for trouble, but neither one of the brothers was close to her Daniel.

Gabe poured her a glass of wine, and she could tell he was dying to ask questions, but he didn't. Unlike Sean, who did nothing but ask her questions until Daniel called him off.

"You're entitled to have tomorrow night off," Gabe said.

Daniel grinned at her. "It doesn't happen often. Don't get used to it, but tomorrow, we'll take shameless advantage of the fact that my brother is a romantic sap. What do you want to do?"

"We'll figure something out," she told him, and he grabbed her hand. Always touching her. She didn't know she was a touchy person. The Montefiores weren't touchy people, but she could get used to this.

In the end, they didn't go anywhere on Saturday. They slept late, he proudly showed her his collection of Rolling Stones albums and she spent the afternoon listening to the strains of "I Can't Get No Satisfaction" and sketching him—in the nude.

"I want you to show a sketch to your mother."

"Of you? I don't think so. You don't know my mother."

"Not me. But one of the other ones. You have a lot of good ones."

"Maybe." She still wouldn't commit, but she was willing to think about it. He did that. Made her think about things that she wouldn't have thought about before.

ON SUNDAY MORNING, Daniel awoke in his bed, his hands reaching out.

There.

He smiled to himself, anticipating the day, anticipating the moment when she would wake up. He loved watching her wake up. He loved her.

She reached out a hand, sliding up and down his back, and her lips curled up in what had to be the world's sexiest smile. A smile meant for him.

When he pulled Catherine into his arms, he kissed her long and lingeringly.

Her brown eyes flickered open, blinking back sleep, her skin soft and bare. "I could get used to this."

"I already am."

"I love you," she whispered, and Daniel murmured a quiet prayer.

"I love you, too. That's why I want to marry you."

"You want to marry me?"

"Yeah. Tell me yes."

He could see her hesitation, and he wanted to shoot himself for jumping too early, but he didn't want to waste a second with her. "I don't know."

It wasn't the answer that he wanted, but he'd been prepared for it.

"Then we wait. And every day, I'll ask you again. Until you know it's right."

"You really mean that?" she asked.

"Hell, yeah. Today's Day One. Will you marry me?"

"I don't know," she said, almost giggling, definitely smiling. Right then, the alarm clock sounded, and he reached over to turn it off, and then noticed the date.

*9/12.*

His smile grew a little broader, and his heart expanded a little bit more.

Honestly, life didn't get any better than this.

# *Epilogue*

CATHERINE WOKE UP the same way she always did. Daniel's hand was on her breast, his thigh thrown across hers and she felt contended. It was getting easier to believe in them now.

She looked at him, studied him—her Odysseus—and smiled. The loneliness was gone from his eyes, his arms weren't empty anymore. She'd done that.

Her.

Catherine Montefiore.

She rose above him, and he slipped inside her, so easily, so sure. He knew her body, knew how to touch her, knew how to please her, and he used that knowledge ruthlessly—ruthlessly being a purely subjective term, of course.

She rode him ruthlessly, a purely subjective term, as well, because he wasn't complaining, either.

Afterward, he held her, never in a hurry to leave, and she liked that time in the morning, when they lay together so comfortably.

"I have something to tell you," he said.

"What?"

"Today is my birthday." She rose up on an elbow and studied his face. He was absolutely, smugly serious.

"You're going to make me pay, aren't you?"

He nodded once. "You aren't going to turn down a man's marriage proposal on his birthday, are you?"

"Did you plan all this out?"

"I had no say on the day of my birth."

She traced a hand down his face. "I love you."

He sighed. "But you still aren't going to marry me, are you?"

Catherine smiled at him, and shook her head. It was time.

She leaned over and kissed him, letting her mouth linger, letting her heart love. "Actually, Daniel, I think I will after all."

\* \* \* \* \*

*Don't miss* Nightcap, *Sean's romance, coming next month from Mills & Boon® Blaze®!*

*Hairdresser Nikki Braxton has had it with dating losers. So when she falls desperately in lust with sexy cowboy Jake McMann, she's thrilled. Jake is the real deal, a man's man. Too bad he's also a vampire...*

*Turn the page for a sneak preview of*

**Dead Sexy**
*by Kimberly Raye,*

*available from Mills & Boon® Blaze®
in October 2009*

### *Dead Sexy*
### *by*
### **Kimberly Raye**

HE NEEDED A WOMAN.

If Jake McCann had been anywhere else in the free world, he would have headed for the nearest singles bar. But he was stuck in the middle of nowhere—aka Skull Creek, Texas—and so he'd headed for its one and only pickup spot: the forty-second annual Founder's Day festival, a weeklong celebration that kicked off with tonight's carnival.

He tipped back the brim of his Stetson and studied his surroundings. The rides had been set up on the ten-acre stretch of gravel parking lot behind the local high school. Pastureland surrounded the area, stretching endlessly in all directions, reminding Jake exactly how far out of his element he really was.

No blinding lights or slabs of concrete. No sirens wailing in the distance or horns honking. Instead he heard the whir of rides, barks of laughter and the cry of a violin from the country two-step that drifted from the large tent at the rear of the carnival, where a battle of the local bands had commenced.

There was a giant Ferris wheel and a brightly lit merry-go-round, along with a few more daring rides. Mad Teacups.

The Whirligig. The Octopus. Booths lined the main strip, offering everything from the chance to knock down a dozen milk cans and win a giant stuffed SpongeBob, to hoop shots for a dollar.

He shifted his attention to the two brunettes who stood munching hot dogs near the ringtoss. His gaze locked with one of them and hunger brightened her eyes. She licked her lips suggestively and lust echoed through him. His gaze caught and held number two, who eyed him with the same blatant interest. Her wedding ring winked as she lifted the hot dog to her lips, and he turned away.

His gaze slid to a pretty blonde who clasped the hand of a young boy and dragged him after her. Her brother. Jake knew it even though he didn't know her.

He could see into her thoughts, taste the frustration in her mouth, feel the displeasure that prickled her skin. She'd been stuck babysitting and she wasn't at all happy about it. She'd wanted to hang with her boyfriend tonight. She'd wanted to…

Jake shook away the thought and hopped off that horse before it could run away with him. He was wired enough on his own without letting someone else's fantasies feed the desire already gripping him tight.

He spotted another woman. A knockout in her late thirties. Married. Mentally counting the seconds until she could slip away from her husband and rendezvous with his brother over by the Haunted House. They'd been seeing each other off and on for the past three years. He'd become an addiction she couldn't do without.

Jake knew the feeling.

He had his own addiction.

His own curse.

Not for long.

He'd searched and watched and waited for the past ten years since discovering the means to free himself, and the time had finally come. In nine days he would escape the hunger that held him captive. He would face his past, his sire, and he would defeat him—and then he would be normal again.

A man rather than a vampire.

If he intended to be victorious, he had to be at the top of his game.

Fully alert.

Physically strong.

Emotionally ready.

*Powerful.*

And there was only one surefire way to beef up his strength—he needed to feed.

Not in the traditional sense. There were some perks to being over one hundred years old—namely he could go days without sinking his fangs into a sweet, succulent female. Contrary to popular myth, the need for blood didn't define him. It was just a part of who he was.

He was also a giant mass of energy.

Tonight's hunt was all about charging that energy. About finding another life force, preferably while it was at its most vibrant, and soaking up the extra voltage.

Tonight's hunt was all about S-E-X.

That's why Jake had left Houston and his motorcycle design business to head for the hill country. He wanted plenty of time to prepare for the coming confrontation. He'd ridden into town just a few hours ago, over a week before his sire was due to return to Skull Creek to relive the turning.

It was what all vampires did on the anniversary of their change. On the exact date, at the exact moment, each was instinctively called back to the site where he or she had left their humanity behind. While reliving the moment of death, a vampire was at his most vulnerable.

Jake had managed to pinpoint the location and he intended to launch his attack while his sire was at his weakest. But he wasn't going to rely on timing alone to guarantee victory.

He'd checked himself into the nearest motel and wasted zero time in heading straight for the one event that offered the biggest selection of females—the carnival that kicked off a weeklong celebration honoring the town's founders. In particular, Sam Black who'd single-handedly fought off a group of Santa Anna's men during the Texas Revolution and preserved the small settlement of Skull Creek.

The man was a legend. A hero.

To everyone but Jake.

He walked toward the ticket booth, looking, sensing, *feeling*. It was another perk of being what he was and the only one he was truly going to miss. Trust had never been a high commodity with the people in his life. Not during the thirty years he'd been human nor in the hundred-plus years since.

Luckily he didn't walk into any situation blindly. He could look into any human's eyes and see their darkest fear, their fondest dream, their deepest desire, their true character. It had saved his ass more than once since he'd been turned and it also kept him from hooking up with the wrong type of woman.

Namely the nice kind. The ones interested in more than a night of hot, wild, steamy sex. The sort who wanted love and marriage and commitment.

All three were impossible for him.

Love? Hell, he'd never been in love with anyone, not when he'd been just a man, and certainly not since he'd turned. He wasn't even sure such a thing existed.

And marriage? Immortality sort of put a crimp in the whole till-death-do-us-part deal.

As for commitment... He had that one down pat, but it didn't involve a female. His dedication centered solely on finding and destroying the vampire who'd turned him back in 1883 and freeing himself once and for all.

Jake's only real potential when it came to the opposite sex involved lots of bone-melting orgasms. That much he could and would guarantee every woman. Rather than deceive anyone, he preferred to be as up-front as possible. Obviously he wasn't anxious to get himself staked, so he kept the vampire part to himself. But his intentions—sex and nothing but sex—he made crystal clear.

*Satisfaction.*

That was the only promise Jake ever made.

The only one he could keep.